INN TOO DEEP

A Wildflower Inn Mystery Book 2

HARPER LIN

This is a work of fiction. Names, characters, organizations, places, events, and incidents are either products of the author's imagination or are used fictitiously.

INN TOO DEEP

ISBN: 978-1-987859-97-3

www.harperlin.com

Chapter 1

The lobby of the Wildflower Inn had just settled into its usual midday quiet when the double doors swung open, letting in a gust of cool autumn air. I had checked in two guests earlier with a polite smile and a cheerful, "Enjoy your stay," and was about to take my afternoon break out by the vineyard, but the lobby came to life with the arrival of two guests.

One of them was a striking older woman. Her heels clicked sharply against the polished wood floor. She had an undeniable presence, like a living, breathing homage to Betty Boop. She was in her fifties, with impossibly large brown eyes framed by heavy liner and lashes that could probably create a breeze if she blinked hard enough. Her bright red dress clung to her figure, and white gloves—yes, gloves—peeked out as she waved a lace fan in front of her face. Her hair was piled high in a beehive that could've been a structural marvel, and the jangling of her half-dozen bracelets filled the room with cheerful clinks as she strolled toward the front desk.

"I'm telling you, it was him! Tinted windows can't fool me. Tinted windows on that rust bucket of a jalopy he was driving. Of course, it was him," she was saying to the tall, broad-shouldered man behind her, who was carrying a couple of vintage suitcases.

"You don't know it was him for sure." His voice was calm, but there was a note of weariness to it, like he'd had this exact conversation before.

The woman waved him off with an impatient flick of her hand. "Who else would try and run us off the road right in the middle of town?" she demanded. Then, as if the thought of it had exhausted her, she fanned herself more vigorously and closed the gap to the counter. Her bracelets jingled merrily, a sharp contrast to the storm cloud on her face.

I straightened and smiled, stepping into my role. "Welcome to the Wildflower Inn."

The woman's expression softened immediately, her dramatic presence shifting into something almost warm. "Hi, honey. You should have a reservation for Geneva Panchella," she said, her voice dropping into a smooth purr. Then she winked.

I blinked, surprised but quick to recover. Geneva Panchella. The name had come up during one of our recent staff meetings—a famous romance novelist staying at the inn for a book tour stop. I pulled up her reservation on the computer and found her name instantly.

"Yes, Ms. Panchella," I said. "You're in the Vineyard Suite. It's one of our nicest rooms—French doors, a small balcony overlooking the vineyard, and a clawfoot bathtub."

She beamed. "Perfect." Then she leaned closer, her bracelets clinking as she placed her elbows delicately on the counter. "And you should also have a room nearby for my trusty sidekick, Mr. Kean Bellow."

I glanced at the screen and nodded. "Yes, ma'am. His room is just across the hallway."

Kean had set the suitcases down by now, his expression unreadable but his presence steady, like a rock in the middle of a stormy sea. I noticed the gold nugget ring on his pinky, a touch that added to the air of mystery about him.

Geneva fanned herself with her lace fan, the motion almost hypnotic as she leaned an elbow on the counter. "That'll work. Do you have a security guard on duty here?" she asked, her tone somewhere between curiosity and concern.

"Well, not an official security guard," I admitted, glancing at Kean, who stood stoically beside her. "But the owners live on the premises. There's always someone around in case of an emergency. Plus, St. Joseph's Hospital is less than ten minutes away if anyone needs medical attention." I paused, trying to gauge her mood. "Is there something I can help you with right away?"

She didn't seem distressed, nor did her bodyguard—or sidekick, or whoever he was. But the question had felt loaded. I must have looked as puzzled as I felt because Geneva sighed dramatically, waving the fan a little faster.

"No, that's not what I mean," she said. Before I could press further, Kean chimed in.

"I'm telling you, it wasn't him," he said, the sigh in his voice mirroring hers but with less patience.

"Maybe I should speak with the manager," Geneva said, directing the comment toward Kean rather than me. For a moment, I thought she'd actually ask to see Max. Instead, Kean's eyes rolled upward in exaggerated exasperation.

"Not now," he said, his voice low but firm. "Let's get you unpacked and settled first. You'll see… it's all in your head."

Geneva's eyebrows shot up as she gave him a withering look. "Oh, yeah? And here I was wondering why I keep you around." She rolled her eyes right back at him, the two of them exchanging what could only be described as a practiced routine. Their banter left me more confused about their relationship than ever. Separate rooms, no rings on their fingers—whatever they were, it wasn't something easily labeled.

Clearing my throat, I slid their keys across the counter. "Is there a problem?" I asked cautiously.

Geneva picked up her key and tilted her head toward me, her bracelets jangling. "Honey, can you do me a favor?" she asked. "If a short fellow with graying curly hair, bad teeth, stupid blue-framed glasses, and a belly that makes him look about eight months pregnant walks in the door looking for me, can you call the police right away?"

I froze, blinking at her. The casual delivery made it sound like she was asking for a wake-up call, but there was an unmistakable edge beneath it. My gaze darted to Kean, whose impassive face gave nothing away, then back to her.

"Are you serious?" I asked, hoping I'd misheard.

"Unfortunately, I am," Geneva said, her fan slowing as she met my eyes. For the first time since her arrival, there was a flicker of something real in her expression—embarrassment, maybe. "Some ex-husbands can't seem to grasp the fact that they're an ex. Do you catch my meaning?"

I did. Far more than I wanted to admit. Memories I'd spent months trying to box away threatened to creep back into my mind. I shoved them down quickly, nodding. "I do," I said softly.

Her lips curled into a faint, knowing smile, as though we'd just exchanged the secret handshake to some exclusive club neither of us wanted to join.

"Not to involve you in too much of my gross personal life," she said, "but we were nearly run off the road just now. I think it might have been him. He's been stalking me since the divorce. Leaving dead birds on my '58 Plymouth Fury. Breaking windows on my garage. Driving past my house a dozen times a day." She clicked her tongue, shaking her head as though trying to shake off the weight of it all. "Funny how, when we were married, he had a dozen better places to be. Now that I've put him out with the trash, he can't leave me alone."

Her words landed heavy, and I didn't know what to say. "I'm sorry," I managed, though it felt inadequate.

She waved it off, her bracelets jingling again. "I shouldn't be unloading this on you. You don't mind, do you?"

"Not at all," I said. "That's why I'm in Sierra Hills." The words slipped out before I could stop them, and I quickly shrugged to deflect the truth of it.

"What's your name, honey?" Geneva asked, tilting her head just enough to give me a good look at those impossibly big, expressive eyes.

"Sophie. Sophie Grant."

"Sophie, you already know I'm Geneva Panchella. Call me Ginny. I'm on my book tour, and I insisted it be part of the deal that I do a reading and Q&A in my hometown. Some people think I'm doing it to be nice. Truth is, I'm doing it for spite. A lot of people in this town thought they had me pegged when I was growing up. You might say I hold a grudge. But I've done signings in smaller towns than this."

"How exciting," I said.

Even though I'd never read her books, from what I'd heard in the staff meeting, Ginny wrote novels so steamy her readers were left with flushed cheeks and, apparently, a need to fan themselves. Her personal life, though, was just as dramatic as her books. She'd already mentioned an ex-husband, but which one? There had been four. I couldn't help it. I was drawn to her like a moth to a flame.

"It's not a big deal," Ginny said, waving her fan dismissively. "I'll be surprised if anyone shows up. The story of a local girl making it big is kind of cliché. Since there will probably be plenty of open seating, you should come. There's a free copy of my latest novel in it for you. You do like to read, don't you?"

I glanced at her, then at Kean, before nodding. "Of course."

She smiled knowingly. "I could tell you're a thinker. Thinkers read. It'll be at Copperstone's Bookstore tomorrow night. Do you know where that is?"

"I do. Thank you, Ginny. I'm looking forward to it."

"Well, that makes one of us," she said with a wink. Then, with a dramatic flourish of her fan, she turned to Kean. "Mr. Bellow, to our rooms."

Just then, Max Amandes walked into the lobby, looking like he'd stepped out of a business magazine in his tailored suit. The sharp angles of the jacket seemed capable of cutting paper. His gaze landed on Ginny.

"Hey, big-and-good-lookin'. Where's the coffee station?" she called out, her voice commanding but playful.

Max didn't miss a beat. "Right that way, ma'am," he said, gesturing down the hallway with a polite smile and a hint of amusement in his eyes.

Kean hoisted the suitcases he'd momentarily set down, nodded in my direction, and followed Ginny. The two of them disappeared down the hall, leaving a faint scent of expensive perfume in their wake.

"Who was that?" Max asked, stepping behind the desk to glance at the computer. The clean, woodsy scent of his cologne made the air feel fresher somehow.

"Geneva Panchella. The author," I said, watching his face closely.

Max's eyes widened in a way I'd never seen before. "That was Geneva Panchella? Wow."

"What do you mean, *wow*?" I asked, a strange twinge blooming in my chest. Ginny was at least twenty years older than Max, but the way he said 'wow' had me overthinking everything. Did he have a thing for older women? Not that it mattered. Just because Max was smart, handsome, and had a knack for checking in on me in a way that felt more personal than professional didn't mean I thought he had an interest in me. Right?

"I knew she wrote romance books," Max said, interrupting my spiraling thoughts. "But I didn't expect her to be so eccentric. You could see her coming a mile away. For some reason, I expected a little old lady in a cardigan and therapeutic shoes. When I spoke to her on the phone, she was bossy. Rude."

I laughed, maybe a little too loud. Relief washed over me. "She didn't say I shouldn't mention this, so I think you should know… she's got someone stalking her."

The humor drained from Max's face. His expression darkened in a way that told me this wasn't the kind of news any inn manager wanted to hear.

"What do you mean?" he asked, his tone serious now.

I told him everything Ginny had shared—her questions about security, the near-accident on the way here, and her vivid description of her ex-husband.

Max pinched his lips together and adjusted his jacket sleeves, the way he always did when he was trying to keep his frustration in check. "See, I knew from the start she was going to be trouble. Just the way she placed her reservation gave me that impression. I don't want this kind of drama here."

"You can't kick her out. She just got here," I said, leaning on the desk. Ginny shouldn't have to leave because of her ex-husband's behavior.

Max exhaled sharply, then nodded. "Fine. I'll let the staff know to keep an eye out for this guy in case he decides to show up around here or sneak onto the premises through the vineyard." He paused. "She drives a 1958 Plymouth Fury?"

"That's what she said," I confirmed.

Max walked over to the window, his hands tucked in his jacket pockets, and looked out at the parking lot. Curious, I hurried around the counter and stood on tiptoes to peek over his shoulder. Sure enough, there it was: a red-and-white 1958 Plymouth Fury parked right outside the front doors. The car practically glowed under the afternoon sun, its polished finish catching the light. Aside from a little dust around the tire wells, it sparkled like it had just rolled off the assembly line.

"They don't make cars like that anymore," Max said, his tone neutral. Then he shook his head, his lips pulling into a tight line. "Nothing like drawing as much attention to yourself as possible when you claim to have a stalker. I'm starting to think this might just be some grand scheme to bolster book sales. I don't like it at all."

I frowned, looking out at the car again. Who would stage something so elaborate? Geneva Panchella already had a name for herself. If she wanted attention, she didn't need a stunt this dramatic to get it. Something about the idea didn't sit right with me. Sure, she was theatrical, but this? This felt different.

"I don't know," I said after a moment. "She seems too established for that kind of ploy. Wouldn't it be something a struggling author might do? Someone who's trying to get noticed?"

Max didn't reply immediately, his expression unreadable as he stared out at the Fury. I glanced at him, then back at the car. My gut told me there was more to Geneva than what she let on. There was a story there, and I intended to learn as much as I could while she was staying at the inn.

"Would you like a car like that?" I asked, trying to lighten the mood. Max didn't strike me as the kind of guy who'd care much about classic cars, but I was curious.

"I don't think it's me," he said with a small smirk. "Would you?"

"Gosh, I don't know. I mean, I can't say it's not pretty." I felt a little self-conscious admitting it, but it was true. The Fury was stunning, more of a work of art than a car. It practically made the vehicles around it disappear into the background, and I wasn't the only one who noticed. People walking by slowed down to get a better look, their heads turning as they passed.

"That it is," Max agreed, his voice thoughtful. Then he turned away from the window and straightened his jacket. "I'll let everyone know what she said about her ex. As for the other guests, how many are left to check in?"

"We've got about twelve. All twenty-four rooms are booked for the weekend," I said, glancing at the reservation list on the computer.

"That's because of her," Max said, jerking his thumb toward the Plymouth outside. "She's doing a book signing and a workshop. She's got a lot of fans. You'd have to, to be a best-selling author." He paused, frowning. "I'm not all that happy about it."

"Why not?" I asked, genuinely puzzled. "We've got a full house."

Max's expression darkened slightly. "In addition to having a possible stalker, she told me she wants to use the Wildflower Inn in her next novel. At least that's what she said over the phone when she made her reservation. I don't think taking the scandals that have happened here over the years and intertwining them with lurid love affairs is going to be good for business."

I blinked, unsure how to respond. To me, the history of the Wildflower was half its charm. Sure, some of it was scandalous, but that's what made it fascinating. People loved stories like that. And if Ginny added a wild romance to the mix, well… it could only make it more interesting. Still, I could see why Max might be concerned. He'd always been protective of the inn's reputation.

"I guess that depends on how she writes it," I said carefully. I wasn't about to admit it, but learning this new tidbit made me even more eager to read the book Ginny promised at her signing. I couldn't wait to see what she'd do with the Wildflower.

Strangely enough, I wasn't the only one at the inn who seemed excited about her stay.

Chapter 2

After I checked most of the other guests in, the front desk phone rang. The digital light blinked, showing it was coming from Ginny's room. I picked up, greeting her cheerfully.

"I'm going to take a snooze," she said without preamble. "Can you give me a wake-up call in about one hour?"

"Of course," I replied.

"Kean will be running errands for me and probably stopping for an afternoon cocktail before coming to fetch me," she continued, sighing dramatically. "He hates when I make him wait. Ugh. Such a man."

I bit back a smile, wondering yet again what

their relationship was. "Yes, ma'am. I'll call you in exactly one hour."

Ginny muttered something I couldn't quite make out before suddenly shouting, "Grazie!" and hanging up. Shaking my head, I quickly set the alarm on the system to ensure the call would go through right on time.

Just then, Jesse ambled up to the counter, his chef's jacket spotless. That trademark grin of his was already in place.

"So, I hear a certain author has checked in," he said.

"Yup, Geneva Panchella is here. She's about to take a nap."

Jesse's eyes lit up. "I love her books."

I blinked at him, taken aback. "What? Really?"

He nodded, clearly amused by my reaction. Jesse, the free-spirited, go-with-the-flow type, didn't exactly strike me as a romance reader. This revelation made him even more intriguing.

"I've read all her books," he said, leaning casually on the counter. "I know, they're kind of chick lit, but the woman tells a good story. Sure, there's some sexy stuff thrown in, but her characters are relatable, her settings are well-described, and her dialogue... it's top-notch."

"Wow, Jesse. Have you ever seen her in person?" I asked.

He shook his head. "Nope."

I grinned. "Well, you won't be able to miss her. She invited me to her book signing event tonight."

"Oh, you lucky dog. I'd tag along, but I've got my Healthy Harvest Organic Cooking class tonight. You know, the kitchen is forever evolving. Can't let the latest eggplant cooking technique pass me by," he teased, winking.

"I'll take notes for you," I offered.

"Great. In the meantime, how about I whip you up something with the leftovers I've got in the kitchen? We wouldn't want anything going to waste," he said with a grin. "Besides, I can't have you turning into skin and bones. You'll eat while I'm on duty, that's for sure."

"Okay," I said, unable to stop smiling.

"You know, you might see my mom at the book signing," Jesse added as I followed him into the kitchen. The remaining staff left after the lunchtime rush. For dinner, the guests went to our formal restaurant in our basement.

Jesse went straight to the fridge, pulling out a few items I couldn't make out, and grabbed a clean pan. The clatter of utensils quickly gave way to the sound of sizzling, and soon the kitchen smelled heavenly.

"Is that how you got into Ginny's books? From your mom?" I asked.

Jesse's grin widened as he shook his head. "Are you kidding? I introduced those books to my mom, not the other way around."

I laughed. "I don't believe you."

Stella Amandes, the matriarch of the family, was the epitome of elegance and grace. She spent her days tending to the wildflower gardens and arranging bouquets for the inn, local restaurants, weddings, and even the town gift shop. It was hard to imagine her enjoying steamy romance novels, but then again, there was always more to people than met the eye.

"Ask her. When you see her tonight at the book signing," Jesse insisted, flipping fresh veggies in a pan with a practiced ease. He turned the contents out onto a pristine white plate, garnished it with a sprinkle of sea salt and pepper, and set it down in front of me.

"What is all this?" I asked, marveling at the vibrant colors of purple potatoes, green onions, yellow peppers, mushrooms, and perfectly wilted spinach with finely chopped meat woven throughout.

"I call it 'what we had on hand,'" he said.

Chuckling, I picked up a fork and took a bite. The flavors exploded in my mouth, warm and harmonious. A subtle hint of cilantro and just enough hot pepper mingled with the rich, earthy taste of the vegetables, all brought together by a drizzle of extra virgin olive oil. It was delicious, better than anything I could've hoped for.

"This is so good," I mumbled through a mouthful, too enamored with the dish to bother with manners.

Jesse's grin widened. "Glad you like it."

"Someday, you'll have to teach me how to cook a few things," I said impulsively, then froze midchew. "Or just write down some simple recipes. That's all I meant," I added quickly, backtracking. "Not literally teach me how to cook. I know you don't have time for that."

"I'm sure I could give you a couple of pointers," he said, clearly amused.

"Yeah. Sure. Just a couple of pointers," I echoed, trying to sound casual as I looked up from my bowl. But his light blue eyes sparkled with humor, and my cheeks warmed under his gaze.

"These pepper flakes are spicy," I blurted, desperate to change the subject.

Thankfully, before I could embarrass myself further, Stella Amandes walked in, a basket of wild-flowers hanging from her arm. She looked as if she'd just stepped out of a foreign film, her white bob slightly windswept, her dress flowing elegantly as she glided across the room.

"Good afternoon, you two," she said, her voice warm as she patted Jesse's cheek on her way past. Of her two sons, Jesse resembled her the most, the same bright blue eyes, the same easy charm, and a shared love of nature. Beneath his toque, his mop of thick blond waves was a near match for her hair, only longer.

"Stella, Jesse was just telling me you're going to Geneva Panchella's book signing tonight. I'm going too," I said.

Stella whirled around, one hand pressed to her chest, her left eyebrow arched. "She's checked in already?"

"Yes, she has," I replied.

"Oh, I wanted to catch a glimpse of her," Stella said, her tone filled with anticipation. "I'll bet she's quiet and reserved, dresses smartly like an older grand dame. Did she wear statement pieces of jewelry? Maybe a cocktail ring or a huge brooch? And I'll bet she has one of those sultry, smoky voices like Lauren Bacall. Have you read any of her novels, Sophie? They're simply wonderful. Just wonderful. I also heard she's considering using the Wildflower as the backdrop for her next story. Can you imagine? Our little inn, immortalized in print."

"No, I haven't read any of her books yet," I admitted. "But she promised me a free copy of her latest if I went to her event tonight."

I could hardly wait to see Stella's reaction when she met Ginny. She was nothing like the image Stella had just painted. But before I could lose myself in that thought, I remembered Ginny's warning.

"There's something I need to tell you both about her," I said, lowering my voice slightly. Both Jesse and Stella leaned in, their expressions turning serious.

A guest with a stalker was dangerous. A guest who was a well-known author with a stalker? That was the kind of story that ended up in a movie, the type where ankles got broken by obsessive fans. I shivered at the thought and quickly relayed Ginny's concerns, describing her ex-husband and the incidents she'd mentioned.

"That's terrible," Stella said, her voice soft with sympathy.

"I'll make sure the evening staff in the restaurant is aware," Jesse said, his light blue eyes darkening with concern.

"Thanks," I said, nodding. I took another bite of my food, grateful for the distraction. Once I'd finished the last delicious spoonful, I returned to the front desk to check in any remaining guests. Afterward, I made the wakeup call to Ginny's room.

Chapter 3

The Copperstone Bookstore sat seven blocks from the inn, tucked at the end of a tree-lined side street with a little parking lot. Ginny's vintage Plymouth was unmistakable, parked off to the rear, its cheerful color contrasting against the otherwise moody setting. The black brick building, framed by black wood windows and a heavy black door trimmed in copper, gave off a brooding charm. It was the kind of charm that had made me fall in love with Sierra Hills in the first place.

Above the bay window, polished copper letters spelled out "Copperstone Bookstore," their edges tinged with green from age and weather. There was something inviting about the place, a vibe that seemed to say, "Come on in and I'll bet you leave with not just a new book or two but a new perspective. Try me."

I adjusted the strap of my purse and smoothed the fabric of my skirt before climbing the two concrete steps. The cement lions on either side of the door watched me pass, their stoic faces adding to the store's whimsical atmosphere. I gave the heavy door a firm yank and stepped inside.

The steady murmur of voices greeted me. It hadn't registered earlier just how many cars had been in the parking lot, but now it was clear Ginny's prediction that no one would show up was completely off the mark. The bookstore was bustling.

I wove my way through small groups of people chatting in pockets throughout the store. Many held tattered copies of Ginny's books, their dog-eared pages and worn covers a testament to loyal readership. Near the center of the room, a large display showcased her novels. I made my way toward it, taking in the daring covers that might even make Fabio blush.

Nine books in total, each one a standalone drama packed into roughly three hundred pages.

Out of genuine curiosity, I picked one up, flipped it over, and started reading the back cover.

Journalist Lina Harper is chasing the story of her career, exposing a corrupt tech billionaire who will do anything to keep his secrets buried. But when she gets too close, she finds herself torn between two men: Alec Ryder, a rugged security specialist with a shadowy past, and Damian Cross, the enigmatic billionaire whose lies she's determined to expose. As sparks fly with both men, Tessa is pulled into a dangerous web of deception, passion, and betrayal. With her heart and her life on the line, Tessa must decide who to trust—and who to destroy. Dangerous Desire *is a steamy, high-stakes love triangle that will leave you breathless.*

People weren't exaggerating when they said her books were scandalous. Just skimming the chapters made me feel like I'd stumbled into a world of intrigue, forbidden love, and drama. But it also left me feeling like a bit of a fraud. I hadn't read a single word of her writing before tonight. This brief description was the most I'd ever consumed from an author with such a huge following.

I resolved then and there that I wasn't going to let Ginny give me a book for free. The least I could do was buy one, a small gesture of gratitude for inviting me to her event. Reaching for my wallet, I felt a light tap on my shoulder. I turned around and looked up about a foot and a half into Kean's serious face.

Ginny saw you come in. She's got a seat for you," Kean said.

"Oh, no. I couldn't," I stammered. "These people have been waiting and standing around, some of them in heels. I don't think it would be…"

Kean took a step back, extending his arm with an air of authority. "Believe me, you'll want a front-row seat for this. And under your chair, you'll find your goodie bag. Just a little something from Ginny to say thanks for coming."

"Oh, gosh. No. I already decided to buy one of her books. I can't take this. It's too…"

"You can. And you will," he said firmly, cutting off my protest. "If you'll excuse me. Oh, by the way, the rooms are perfect. Just what we needed."

I offered a hesitant smile, still unsure what to make of Kean and his relationship with Ginny. They weren't quite like brother and sister. But they also weren't a couple. The mystery of their connection lingered in the back of my mind as I took a deep breath and sat down in the aisle seat marked "Reserved."

Beneath my chair, I found a gift bag, which I placed on my lap and peeked inside. It held a signed copy of Ginny's latest book, a whimsical bookmark featuring an English bulldog in a bumblebee costume, a small spiral notebook stamped with the words "What I Read," and a bright yellow pen with a black tassel. It was a thoughtful gesture, and I felt a little giddy. I glanced at my watch—still fifteen minutes until the event officially started.

Looking around the room, I offered a polite smile to a few people who noticed I'd been ushered to the VIP section. The bookstore's layout caught my eye. A staircase led to a second floor, and I was fairly certain there was a third. Just as I was about to admire my goodie bag again, movement at the edge of the seating area caught my attention.

Ginny's words echoed in my head: *"If a short fellow with graying curly hair, bad teeth, stupid blue-rimmed glasses, who looks about eight months pregnant walks in the door looking for me, can you call the police right away?"*

There he was. A man fitting that description stood near the edge of the crowd, shifting nervously. From my seat, I couldn't confirm the bad teeth—he wasn't smiling—but everything else matched: short, gray hair, blue glasses, and a round belly straining against his sweater. His forehead glistened with sweat, and his darting eyes suggested he was more interested in the people around him than the book-shelves he pretended to browse.

I slipped my goodie bag back under my chair and stood, trying to casually circle the seating area while keeping him in my line of sight. He mingled awkwardly among the clusters of people, feigning interest in the books but clearly more focused on surveying the room.

My thoughts raced. Ginny's ex-husband didn't fit the dashing, mysterious archetypes in her novels, but there had to be something about him that once caught her attention. Maybe he was funny or wealthy. Maybe he was brilliant but socially inept. Whatever the reason, their relation-ship had ended, and now he was skulking around a crowded bookstore. His behavior was creepy, and I couldn't shake the unease prickling the back of my neck.

Before I could get any closer, a voice came over the loudspeaker. "Anyone here to attend the reading and book signing for Geneva Panchella, please take your seats. We will begin in five minutes. Thank you."

The man froze, his head snapping toward the announcement. As I stepped forward, a huge shadow passed behind me. Kean. His tall frame moved quickly through the crowd, zeroing in on the man.

"No! No!" the man shouted, throwing up a hand as though to stop a train.

"You aren't supposed to be here, David," Kean said, his voice low but commanding. "You know it. Now we can do this quietly without any drama, or I can literally toss you out of here."

David's eyes darted toward the largest group of people, his expression shifting to something almost gleeful. His voice rose, drawing attention. "Don't you touch me! I have every right to be here. This is a public place. Do you hear me, Kean? A public place!"

As the crowd reacted with murmurs, I edged closer, watching as Kean tried to reason with him, but David was having none of it. He was relishing the growing crowd, clearly enjoying the scene he was causing.

"Tell her I've forgiven her. It will all be all right. I'm ready to take her back, and I'll pretend the whole thing never happened. Go on, Kean. Tell her for me. That's a good errand boy." David's tone dripped with condescension.

Kean took a sudden step forward, and David flinched, nearly jumping out of his skin. Kean let out a laugh, a low, deliberate sound that clearly unnerved the smaller man.

"David, you know you're not supposed to be here. There's a restraining order. You don't want me to call the police and press charges. You know they'll stick," Kean said, his voice calm but firm. "You don't have any business being in Sierra Hills, let alone this bookstore."

"I have every right to be here," David snapped, his voice rising. "Every right!" He began backing away, his eyes darting wildly around the store.

Before I could process what was happening, David was speed-walking through the bookstore, with Kean close behind. My instincts told me to follow, though I kept a safe distance in case things escalated. I didn't want to get caught in the middle if David decided to cause a scene.

The chase was almost surreal, like something out of an old slapstick comedy. David ducked behind bookshelves, slipped past the information counter, and finally found himself cornered between a rack of maps and a towering display of atlases.

"Just let me talk to her. She's my wife," David said, his voice cracking as he put his hands together in a pleading gesture. From my vantage point behind a shelf of travel guides, I had a clear view of the standoff.

"She's your ex-wife. Has been for over eight months now," Kean replied, his tone steady as he slowly advanced. "And you're leaving. Now."

David's shoulders slumped, his whole body seeming to collapse in on itself. He looked like a deflated balloon, all the bravado draining out of him. "She's lied to you," he mumbled. "Everything she says is a lie."

"Stop, David," Kean said, his voice tinged with exasperation.

"You know she's lying. You know it! She lies about everything!" David's voice rose again, frantic and uneven.

Kean let out a long sigh, his patience clearly wearing thin. "David, I'm giving you until the count of three," he said through clenched teeth.

"And you'll do what? You can't touch me. I have every right to be here. All I want is five minutes to talk to her," David whined, his voice teetering on the edge of a tantrum.

"You need to stop following her. Stop calling her. Stop threatening and harassing her," Kean said, his tone like a cold blade. "Now, you've got a choice. Either you leave quietly, or I call the cops. Which is it?"

For a moment, David actually seemed to consider his options, his bewildered expression giving way to a grimace of anger. A pit formed in my stomach as I watched, a wave of déjà vu washing over me. I'd been here before. Not exactly here, not in a bookstore, but in a grocery store, with my own ex shadowing me through the aisles. Back then, I didn't have someone like Kean to stand up for me. I'd left my cart and fled.

"This isn't over," David spat, his face twisting with rage. He turned and stormed toward the front door, nearly ripping it off its hinges as he shoved it open. For a little guy, he was surprisingly strong, and clearly furious.

Kean rubbed a hand over his bald head, then massaged the back of his neck before turning back toward the event area. I sidled up to him, concern etched across my face.

"Are you all right?" I asked softly.

He glanced down at me, his expression a mix of weariness and irritation. "Don't tell Ginny he was here. She'll have an episode, a conniption, or something worse. We're not planning to stay in town long. A week tops. I'm going to suggest we leave sooner rather than later."

"I'm so sorry," I said, my voice barely above a whisper.

"Thanks," Kean replied gruffly. "I'm going to make sure he's actually gone. Go back to your seat. Everything's fine."

"Are you sure you don't want the manager to call the police?" I pressed gently.

Kean shook his head. "No. I'll handle it. Just go on." His gaze was firm, leaving no room for argument.

I nodded and made my way back to the seating area, though my mind was racing. Why wouldn't he want Ginny to know David had been there? She'd already guessed he was the one who'd tried to run her off the road. But Kean knew her better than I did, and I had to trust his judgment... for now.

When I returned to my seat, I noticed my goodie bag was gone. I glanced around, about to ask if anyone had seen who might have taken it, but the manager stepped up to the podium, followed closely by Ginny. The moment was lost. Too late now.

Chapter 4

Geneva Panchella looked even more outrageous standing at the small wooden podium than she had when she first arrived at the inn. Her dress was a shimmering gold number that cinched at the waist and flared dramatically, making her every movement seem larger than life. A bright red flower adorned her hair, and she wore matching gloves and heels so high I was certain she needed an oxygen mask. But as soon as she began to read, all of that faded away.

"This is one of my favorite passages," Ginny said, her voice rich and confident. "The heroine has just been betrayed, not only by her lover but by someone she considered her closest friend. I'm sure you all can relate on some level."

She was right. As she began to read, the room fell silent, captivated. The heroine's discovery that her so-called best friend had been sabotaging her all along was devastating. Ginny brought the emotions to life, her delivery layered with a depth that could only come from someone who had lived through such heartbreak. The pain in the story was palpable, and I felt it like a knot in my chest. That was the mark of a good author, to make you forget where you were and fully immerse you in someone else's world.

In that moment, Ginny wasn't the gaudy, eccentric writer I'd first met. She was a woman unapologetically herself, bold and fearless, no matter how over-the-top she might appear. It made me all the more annoyed about my stolen goodie bag. The signed book inside it now felt like a lost treasure, and I couldn't wait to get my hands on something she'd written.

The reading ended to a wave of applause and a few whistles. Since I was sitting at the end of the front row, Ginny looked directly at me, giving me a playful wink and a wave before turning back to the crowd.

"I'm glad you all managed to stay awake," she

joked, earning a ripple of laughter. "Thank you. Now, I'll hand things over to you. Any questions?"

About half a dozen hands shot up. Ginny pointed to someone near the back, a small, birdlike young woman clutching a notebook and pen. She couldn't have been older than eighteen.

"Do you have a process or rituals when you sit down to write?" the girl asked, her voice eager.

Ginny's smile widened. "Are you in a writing class?" The girl nodded shyly. "Every writer has a process that's as individual as a fingerprint. If covering yourself in butter and rolling in Rice Krispies helps you get the words on the page, do it. You'll find your way."

The audience laughed, and Ginny's eyes scanned for the next question. She pointed to an older man holding a cowboy hat, dressed in jeans and a belt buckle big enough to double as a dinner plate.

"Yes, ma'am," he drawled. "When did you realize you wanted to be a writer? Do you think it's ever too late for someone to start a novel?"

Ginny's eyes twinkled. "Hmmm… asking for a friend, right?" The crowd chuckled, and the man tipped his hat good-naturedly. "Look, I wanted to be a writer after I got fired from my seventh job in three years. I've never been good at playing on the playground with the other kids. You strike me as the kind of guy who doesn't give two licks what anyone thinks. If you put characters on the page who look and sound like you, it won't matter how old you are. Are you married?"

"Yes, ma'am. My wife is right over there," he said, pointing to a woman across the room who looked less than amused at the interaction.

Ginny winked at her. "Oh, that's too bad. I'm in the market for number five and... hey, you don't know unless you ask." The audience erupted into laughter. "Come to my workshop at the library tomorrow, and maybe we can get you started... on your novel, that is."

Even I couldn't help but laugh. How could she say things like that out loud? How could she be so bold? As the laughter subsided, Ginny pointed to another woman seated just behind me to the right. She was bouncing slightly on her toes, her excitement palpable, and a massive duffle bag rested at her feet.

"I just love your work, Miss Panchella. I've read every one of your books at least a dozen times. My question for you is, what makes a good writer?"

"That's kind of a broad question," Ginny said,

her tone playful but thoughtful. "Look, I don't like science fiction. So, nothing anyone writes in that genre holds much interest to me. But that doesn't mean those stories are bad just because I don't enjoy them, or good just because you might. I guess, as long as there's a little suffering on the page, a speck of reality that really hurts, that's what makes a good writer." She paused and gave a theatrical shrug. "And that's why I write romance. Suffering comes with the territory. It's easy. Most of the time, it's self-inflicted. Don't we all just love to be miserable sometimes?"

The woman who had asked the question beamed, reaching into her bag to jot notes. It was clear Ginny's words had struck a chord. I admired Ginny's ability to connect with her audience.

Ginny scanned the room for another question, and that's when a deep, abrasive voice rang out from the back.

"Miss Panchella. When you write about suffering, do you take it from the suffering *you* cause people?"

The room froze. Heads swiveled in unison to find the source of the comment. But I already knew. It was David. Somehow, he'd slithered back into the bookstore when no one was looking. My heart sank. Where was Kean? Where was security?

Ginny shook her head, exhaling loudly into the microphone. "Oh, brother. Ladies and gentlemen, my ex-husband," she announced, her voice dripping with disbelief. She stepped back from the podium as the bookstore manager hurried to her side. They exchanged hurried whispers before Ginny turned and made a beeline for the office at the back of the store.

"Gin-Gin! I still love you! I LOVE YOU!" David shouted, his voice cracking. The office door slammed shut behind her. Within moments, security and Kean appeared, sprinting in David's direction. David turned on his heel and bolted, weaving through the aisles like a rat scrambling for cover. He barreled through the front doors, nearly unhinging them as he fled into the night. Security followed close behind, but the commotion finally settled after a few minutes.

The bookstore manager stepped up to the podium, her expression tight. "Ladies and gentlemen, I want to assure you the situation is under control. Miss Panchella will be signing books shortly at the table in the back. We also have copies of her latest novel available for purchase."

The manager's tone was polite, but I could see the strain behind her eyes. I felt a pang of sympathy for Ginny. How humiliating. My own ex-boyfriend had a habit of showing up where I least expected him, and I knew all too well how mortifying it could be. I shook off the memory and refocused on the scene in front of me.

When Ginny finally emerged from the office, she looked as though she'd been crying. Her mascara had smudged slightly at the corners of her eyes, but she held her chin high as she approached the signing table. A pyramid of her latest book stood next to a stack of thick black markers.

"All right, folks. For my second act, I'll be shooting myself out of a cannon," she quipped, her voice steady but tinged with exhaustion. "But first, let's get some books signed so you can all have an exciting story to tell your families."

I stayed in my seat, letting the diehard fans approach first. Belt-Buckle Man was busy trying to calm his wife, who looked ready to boil over. The last thing Ginny needed was another confrontation. When the line finally thinned, I made my way to the table.

"So, how did you like it?" Ginny asked, offering me a tired but genuine smile.

"It was fun. I'm sorry about all the drama. There's just no reasoning with some people, I guess," I said, instantly regretting my choice of words.

Ginny waved it off. "It's not your fault. I just don't understand him. He wasn't like this when we got married. It's like he gave up on being the man I thought he was. I think he just liked my money." Her voice wavered, and I caught the glint of a tear in her eye. My heart ached for her.

"There are people who love what you are but can't handle not having it themselves," I said softly. "Instead of embracing it, they start to resent you for it. I… I know how you feel." Without thinking, I reached out and patted her hand.

Ginny's lips quirked into a smile as she quickly dabbed at her eyes. "Did you like your goodie bag?"

I winced. "I loved it, but when I got up to follow Kean, someone swiped it."

"What?" Ginny's eyes widened in disbelief. "I have a thief for a fan? Ugh. This night cannot get any more embarrassing." She rolled her eyes, and despite everything, I chuckled. Even her exasperation was amusing.

"It's the thought that counts," I said, trying to console her.

"No. That yellow pen was exclusive," she insisted. "A friend of mine makes them in a shade called Tulip Yellow. Oh, if that doesn't just take the cake." She shook her head, then grabbed a copy of her book from the pyramid. Without hesitation, she uncapped a marker and scrawled a message on the title page before signing her name with a flourish. She handed the book to me with a wink.

I was about to thank her when Kean appeared, his expression grim. The bookstore was nearly empty, and the faint chime of the intercom indicated closing time.

"Gin. We've got a problem," he said, shaking his head.

Ginny groaned, throwing her hands in the air. "What could possibly go wrong now?"

"It's the car," Kean said, his jaw tight as he shook his head. His lips pressed into a firm line, and a twitch flickered at the corner of his right eye. His fists clenched at his sides.

With a deadpan expression, Ginny stood and stomped toward the door, Kean close behind her. I hurried after them, my heart pounding. Out in the parking lot, the problem wasn't immediately obvious, but as we approached the Plymouth Fury, the damage came into painful focus. The windshield was shattered, deep scratches marred the gleaming paint, and one of the tires sagged, completely flat.

"That son of a b…!" Ginny spat, her voice seething with rage.

"Now, wait a second, Gin," Kean said, placing a steadying hand on her shoulder. "I'm telling you, I put David in a cab."

Ginny shrugged off his hand. "You don't think he could have come back?"

"He gave me his word he wouldn't," Kean replied, his tone firm.

"He gave me his word he'd forsake all others, and that didn't happen either," she snapped, planting a hand on her hip.

My jaw nearly dropped. David? That guy? He cheated on Geneva Panchella? She wasn't good enough for him? Clearly, he was unhinged. Ginny was funny, smart, and unapologetically herself. If David couldn't appreciate that, he was more than a little nuts.

Before I could voice my thoughts, a squad car pulled into the parking lot. Kean must have already called the police. A uniformed officer stepped out of the driver's side, followed by a familiar face from the passenger side. Detective J.T. Connor. The sight of him made me feel strangely nervous, as if I'd somehow been complicit in the vandalism.

Detective Connor's sharp green eyes scanned the parking lot, pausing briefly on the Fury. His broad chest rose and stayed expanded, his shock evident even through his professional demeanor. He approached, introducing himself to Ginny and Kean, but when his gaze shifted to me, I saw the faint flicker of recognition.

"Miss Grant," he said evenly. "Surprised to see you here."

"I was here for the book signing," I said, my voice embarrassingly small. Could I sound any nerdier?

Connor nodded, then instructed Ginny and Kean to recount what had happened to the uniformed officer while he studied the car. He examined the tires, peered inside, and even crouched to look underneath. Meanwhile, Ginny explained David's earlier outburst and the restraining order. Kean reiterated that he had personally ensured David left in a cab and swore the man had promised not to return.

Ginny folded her arms across her chest, and Kean put a protective arm around her shoulders. She rested her head against him, the gesture both tender and puzzling. What exactly was their relationship? It was sweet, but it only deepened the mystery of their connection.

After a few more minutes, the uniformed officer finished taking notes, and Detective Connor handed Ginny his card.

"If anything else happens, or if you have questions, don't hesitate to contact me," he said. Then his gaze flicked between Ginny and me in a way that made my stomach flip. What was that for? He knew I wasn't going anywhere.

"I have one question," Ginny said, her tone sharp. "Do you know a good body mechanic who can fix my car?"

For the first time, Connor's stern facade cracked. He glanced at the uniformed officer and nodded. "Call Maverick's Body Shop. Tell them to send a truck and mention my name."

The officer made the call, and within minutes, he returned with a bit of good news. "They're sending a pickup truck. They'll assess the damage and let you know."

Ginny let out a long breath and leaned into Kean, who gave her shoulder a comforting squeeze. She glanced up at him with a small smile and a shake of her head before turning her attention to me.

"You said you walked here?" she asked, one hand on her hip.

"Yup," I replied.

"Well, the heck with that. Kean, get us a cab."

Before I could protest, I found myself crammed into the back seat of a cab between Ginny and Kean, feeling like a kid caught in a whirlwind of relatives I barely knew. Ginny wasted no time recounting the theft of my goodie bag, which seemed to irritate Kean even more than the vandalism.

"We'll get you taken care of, Sophie. Don't worry," Kean said, his tone firm.

"It's not a big deal. I'm grateful for the book," I began, but Ginny cut me off.

"I knew there'd be trouble coming back to this town," she muttered, clicking her tongue. "Sierra Hills has never been fair to me." She stared out the window, her expression a mix of nostalgia and defiance. "When you come to the writing workshop tomorrow at the library, I'll have a new goodie bag for you. You're coming, right?"

"I... I didn't know there was one," I stammered.

"There is. Seven o'clock at the Sierra Hills

Public Library. I'll expect to see you there. Kean, make sure she's on the list. Is the library far from the Wildflower Inn?"

"Maybe seven blocks in the other direction," I said, though I wasn't entirely sure. I hadn't been to the library yet but knew it was nearby.

"Too far," Ginny declared. "Kean, arrange for a loaner car."

"Of course," he said, staring out the window.

"It's amazing everything that went on in this town when I was growing up here. Not much has changed. That's too bad."

Ginny's smirk reminded me of Scarlett O'Hara walking into a party after a scandal. There was so much more to her than her roguish novels hinted at, and I wondered what other secrets she carried.

Chapter 5

Considering all the excitement, I fell asleep as soon as my head hit the pillow. I hadn't yet found myself an apartment, so I was using one of the inn's smaller rooms. It wasn't much, but since leaving the city and all the baggage that came with it—both literal and figurative—I'd learned to live simply.

After showering and dressing, I headed downstairs to grab a quick bite. Jesse was already cooking in the kitchen, and I was hoping he'd have something warm and hearty ready. But as I approached, I heard raised voices coming from inside. Max, Jesse, and Stella were having what sounded like a good old-fashioned argument.

I hesitated in the doorway, unsure if I should

walk in or wait. Their conversation was heated, and I didn't want to intrude.

"Mom, it's not a good idea," Max's voice was firm, his frustration palpable. "You see the kind of luck that follows this woman around? If we let her use the inn as a backdrop for her next book, it'll be like leaving cheese out and expecting the rats to stay outside. It's only a matter of time before it comes back to bite us."

"Max, you're being unreasonable," Jesse countered. "Something like this could really put the Wildflower on the map. The place already has an exciting history."

"Exciting?" Max's voice sharpened. "There were extramarital affairs. Counterfeiting. Oh, and let's not forget the murder."

"That we know of," Jesse quipped, a sly grin audible in his tone. "Sounds like all the ingredients for a bestseller. Why shouldn't we enjoy some of the residual popularity that comes with it? People love a good scandal, and…"

"And nothing," Max interrupted, his tone final. "I'm against it. So much so that I think we should tell Geneva Panchella to find other accommodations. Let her use another hotel in her next novel."

A lump formed in my chest at his words. Max

couldn't order Ginny to leave. Not after everything she'd been through. Nearly getting run off the road when she arrived, her ex-husband showing up to humiliate her, and the vandalism to her beloved car. Hadn't she endured enough? Besides, where would she go on such short notice? She'd never find a room as nice as our suite.

"You'll do no such thing, Maximillian," Stella cut in, her voice calm but commanding.

"Mom," Max began, his tone softening slightly, though his determination didn't waver. "I'm the manager of this hotel now. I'm only thinking of what's best and safest for everyone involved. Geneva Panchella isn't our only guest. If someone gets hurt because of her, we could be in serious trouble."

"She's only staying for another day or two, right? What's the point of making her leave?" Jesse asked.

My chest tightened further. Clearly, they hadn't heard about her ordeal last night or the vandalism done to her car. I couldn't avoid it any longer. It was time to step into the middle of this family debate.

I cleared my throat to announce my presence, then walked in with what I hoped was a neutral expression, as if I hadn't overheard a single word.

"Good morning," I said brightly, looking around at each of them.

"Good morning," Jesse greeted me with his signature wide smile.

"How are you this morning, Sophie?" Stella asked warmly.

"Fine, considering all the excitement last night," I replied, deliberately dropping the hint to steer the conversation where it needed to go. I figured this was the best way to bring up what had happened without making it sound like a reason to send Ginny packing.

Max's brow furrowed. "What excitement?" he asked, the only one not smiling.

"Ginny's ex-husband showed up at her book signing," I began, keeping my voice steady. "They think he vandalized her car—smashed the windshield, flattened a tire, and scratched the paint. The police had to be called." I crossed my arms and rocked back on my heels, waiting for their reactions.

Max looked at his mother and brother, his frown deepening. "See what I mean? She's got a crazy person after her. I think she might be a little bonkers herself."

"That's terrible," Stella said, her voice tinged with concern. "We can't turn her out, Max."

"Is she all right?" Jesse asked, echoing my own worries.

"Yes," I said. "A little embarrassed by the whole spectacle, but she's holding up. Her car is in the shop, and she still has to lead her writing workshop tonight. That's a lot of pressure for one person."

I glanced at Max, who had shoved his hands deep into the pockets of his trousers, his gaze fixed on the floor.

"Max?" Stella prompted gently. He looked up at her, his chin still low.

"I don't like this," he admitted, his voice quieter but no less resolute. His eyes flicked between his mother and Jesse. "She married a guy who acts like this? She had to have known he was a nut."

The words stung, even though they weren't directed at me. Memories of my own past resurfaced—the realization, too late, of the kind of person my ex-boyfriend had become. I hadn't known what manipulation looked like until I was drowning in it. Max's judgment felt harsh, even if it wasn't personal.

"Look," Jesse interjected, his tone steady, "the only things we know about her are that she's an author, she wants to use our inn in her next novel, and she's dealing with a domestic issue. That doesn't make her worth throwing out."

Max straightened, his lips pressed into a hard line. "I think she's a liability to the inn and could be a danger to the other guests. I'll agree to let her stay, but again, if something else happens, she'll have to go. And another thing: she is not to use the Wildflower Inn in any of her writing. She does not have permission to do that."

Stella opened her mouth to object, but Max raised a hand to stop her. "I'll make that demand formal," he said, his tone clipped. "She won't have any excuse to misunderstand my intentions."

With that, Max stomped out of the kitchen, heading in the direction of his office. Jesse and Stella exchanged a look, then shrugged as if to say, *What can you do?*

"How about some breakfast, Sophie? I could whip you up something quick," Jesse offered, his easygoing demeanor returning. It was as if he were already certain everything would work out: no more violence, no more disruptions. Ginny would stay without further incidents.

I wished I could share his optimism. As it was, my appetite had completely vanished.

Chapter 6

I arrived at the Sierra Hills Public Library around 6:45. Small groups of people stood around chatting in cliques, their excitement palpable. Scanning the room, I spotted a few familiar faces—Belt-Buckle Man was there, though thankfully without his wife, and the young woman who had gushed about reading Ginny's books a dozen times. No sign of David, thank goodness. Letting out a quiet sigh of relief, I made my way to the front desk and asked where the workshop was being held.

"Are you enrolled?" the woman behind the desk asked, her tone brisk.

"Uh, I think she put me on the list?" I gave her my name. She ran a bony finger down the clipboard in front of her, nodded curtly, and handed me a shiny yellow folder with a sticker that read Geneva Panchella Writing Workshop.

"Thank you," I said, but she only nodded and pointed toward a closed door. The workshop was inside. Trying to stay inconspicuous, I made my way over, but before I could slip through, Ginny's number one fan from the book signing caught sight of me.

"Weren't you at the book signing yesterday?" she asked, her wide smile all teeth.

"Yes, I was," I replied, straightening my shoulders and lifting my chin. She wasn't unpleasant, but her intensity made me self-conscious.

"My name is Corine Schofield," she said, extending a hand. I shook it politely.

"Sophie. Nice to meet you."

"You, too. You were sitting in one of the reserved seats. Are you a reporter?" Corine asked, her curiosity unrelenting.

"Oh, no. Not at all. I work at the Wildflower Inn," I said.

"You do?" Corine said, placing a hand on her hip.

Before the conversation could continue, we were ushered into the event room, where chairs were arranged in a semicircle. At the front of the room stood Ginny, dressed in yet another outfit reminiscent of Mae West. Her boldness was enviable, or maybe Geneva Panchella's style was just plain tacky. Either way, I couldn't help but adore her unapologetic flair.

We all took our seats. Corine maneuvered her way into the chair right next to Ginny, practically vibrating with excitement. She reminded me of an eager puppy, thrilled to be so close to her idol. I ended up between Belt-Buckle Man and an older woman with a cane and a bucket hat.

Nearly everyone in the room had a notebook or a manuscript in hand, pages filled with stories they'd been laboring over for weeks, months, or even years. I felt completely out of place. Writing anything beyond a grocery list had never crossed my mind, yet here I was, attending a bestselling author's workshop.

The event began with introductions. At first, it felt stiff and formal, like being in a classroom where a test might be lurking at the end. But that atmosphere quickly melted away when Ginny asked people to share snippets of their work.

The first volunteer was an older woman who looked like someone's grandma. Her kind face and comfortable outfit exuded warmth, but when she began to read from her handwritten yellow pad, the story she shared was anything but cozy. It was a gritty murder mystery set in a small town, centered on an alcoholic sheriff struggling to solve a grisly crime while battling his own demons. The vivid details of the crime scene and the sheriff's hangover painted a dark, compelling picture.

Her name was Enid. A grandmother of six and great-grandmother of fifteen, she explained that writing gruesome, nail-biting crime stories had been her lifelong dream, and now she finally had the time to pursue it.

Ginny leaned forward, her expression genuinely encouraging. "Have you taken any writing courses?" she asked. "Do you have favorite authors you find yourself mimicking? Do you watch true crime shows?"

Enid shook her head but looked intrigued.

"All of those things will help you," Ginny said. "Take some writing classes here at the library or at the junior college over on Banks Road. Find the authors who write these kinds of stories and read everything they've written. Then read who they like. Before you know it, the jargon, the body language, the grittiness of the genre will become second nature. That means your readers will see your vision clearly."

Enid nodded, her wrinkled hands steady as she scribbled notes. Ginny's words were simple but inspiring, and I could tell they resonated deeply. I felt a spark of admiration for Ginny. Beneath the flamboyant outfits and brash humor was someone who truly cared about helping others find their voice.

Once the ice was broken, the floodgates opened. Attendees eagerly took turns sharing their work, and it quickly became clear I might be stuck here well into the night. Ginny's approachable nature and sharp advice had the room buzzing with energy. That is, until Belt-Buckle Man took the floor.

I knew deep down I wasn't a writer. I loved to read, but the thought of describing scene after scene, developing characters, and crafting dialogue —all while keeping a coherent storyline—felt like too much pressure. Still, I admired the dedication of the people around me. These were storytellers in the truest sense, baring pieces of themselves through their work.

But as Belt-Buckle Man, who introduced himself as Pete Larson, stood up with a manuscript that rivaled *War and Peace* in thickness, I braced myself. My first thought was: *Please don't read the whole thing.*

Pete cleared his throat and began. The room shifted almost immediately. His story was painstakingly descriptive, down to the buttons on a character's shirt and the exact texture of a boot smudge. The dialogue was stilted, the pacing excruciating. I fidgeted in my seat and noticed I wasn't alone. A wave of discomfort rippled through the group.

"Okay, let me stop you right there, Pete," Ginny interrupted after a few minutes, her tone calm but firm. "Is your manuscript finished?"

"Yes. I've got a couple agents I'll be sending it to and…"

"They're going to use it to heat their houses this winter," Ginny said bluntly, cutting him off. "It's too much. Take it home and cut at least half of it. At least. You'll have a much better book, I promise."

Pete bristled. "But you barely let me read anything."

"I didn't need to hear more to know you have a lot of words on the page, but the substance is buried. That's a common mistake for first-time writers."

"You don't know what you're talking about," Pete growled, his face turning red.

Ginny raised an eyebrow and smirked. "Pete, this workshop is about constructive criticism and honest feedback. Learning to handle it is a crucial part of the process."

"This is ridiculous! Who do you think you are, telling me to trash my novel?" Pete snapped.

Ginny remained unfazed. "I didn't say that. If that's what you heard, there might be a bigger issue at hand."

"I can't believe this," Pete ranted. "First, you sexually harass me at your book signing in front of my wife, and now this! I demand my money back!"

Ginny's chuckle was dry, her composure intact. "There are no refunds. You got the critique you requested. If you want to stay for the rest of the workshop, I've got a mini-tutorial on editing prepared that you might find helpful. But you're under no obligation to stay."

Pete's voice rose to a near shout. "This is a scam! You're a scam artist! That's what you are! You'll be hearing from my lawyer. Don't think you can get out of it. I have witnesses!"

"Witnesses to what, Pete?" Ginny asked, her tone biting. "To an established writer giving advice to a rookie? I'll await your summons. Hopefully, it reads better than your manuscript."

Before anyone could respond, Pete's wife stormed in from nowhere, her face a mask of fury.

"Who do you think you are, talking to my husband like that? Just because he rebuffed your come-on doesn't mean you can treat him this way!" she spat.

Ginny rolled her eyes and sighed dramatically. "You've both taken up enough of everyone's time. Please leave."

"We're leaving!" Pete shouted as his wife glared at Ginny. "You call yourself an author? You're nothing but a smut-peddling hack!"

Kean, who had been quietly reading in the back of the room, rose and walked to the door, holding it open for the couple. His calm demeanor was a stark contrast to their stormy exit. As soon as the door shut behind them, Kean gestured for Ginny to continue.

The room buzzed with shock. I glanced around, meeting the wide-eyed stares of other attendees. No one had expected such drama, least of all me. I'd thought a writing workshop would be subdued, a room full of introverts talking about their cats. I couldn't have been more wrong.

Ginny sighed, smoothing her dress. "Ladies and gentlemen, it seems this is turning into my drama tour." The room chuckled. "Was I cruel in Pete's critique? You'd tell me if I was, right?"

Everyone murmured reassurances that she had handled the situation professionally.

"Sometimes, the truth hurts," Corine piped up, practically leaning into Ginny's ear. "This workshop has been fantastic. Truly enlightening."

Ginny's smile softened. "Well, that's encouraging. Thank you." She launched back into her lesson, and by the end of the night, I had to admit I was bitten by the writing bug. Part of me thought, *Why not?* Another part of me thought, *Who do you think you are? Hemingway?* I tucked the idea away for later and approached Ginny to thank her, but my attempt was thwarted.

"Can I help you with anything, Miss Panchella? Do you need anything carried to your car? Would you like another bottle of water?" Corine asked, her wide eyes practically sparkling with admiration.

"No, thank you. The workshop ran a little later than expected, so you go on home. I'm glad you attended," Ginny said graciously.

Kean stepped forward, grabbed her bag, and waited patiently while Ginny shook hands with the remaining attendees, the librarians, and finally Corine one last time. I wouldn't have been surprised if Corine vowed never to wash her hand again.

As we left the building and walked toward the loaner car the mechanic had provided while Ginny's Plymouth was in the shop, I sensed she was a little off. At first, I thought it might be lingering frustration over Pete's outburst, but I stayed quiet, letting her bring it up when she was ready. It didn't take long.

"I think there's something in the water in this town," Ginny said with a dramatic sigh. "I've thought it my whole life. As if it wasn't enough having David nearly run us off the road and show up to make a scene, now Pete—the next great American novelist—throws a fit over a little criticism. I should just retire."

Kean chuckled. "You say that after almost every event, whether it goes well or not."

"I thought both events were amazing," I chimed in.

"You, my dear, are easily amused," Ginny teased, giving me a playful pinch on the arm. "You riding with us back to the hotel? You may as well since your room's there too."

"How did you know that?" I asked, surprised.

"I overheard Max mentioning it to Stella. What a nice woman she is. I agreed to give her a private tutoring session for a small fee and to look over a short story she's been working on," Ginny said as I opened the front passenger door for her. She climbed in slowly, her exhaustion evident. The color in her cheeks had faded, and her eyelids drooped. Who would have guessed being a writer could be so taxing?

"Thanks. I'll join you," I said, happy to accept. I didn't feel like walking back to the inn.

"Oh, Kean. I forgot my jacket inside. Would you mind?" Ginny asked as Kean loaded a few things into the back of the car.

"I'll get it," I offered quickly. Ginny thanked me, and I hurried back into the library. Corine was still there, clutching Ginny's jacket as if it were a prized possession.

"I came back for the jacket," I explained.

"I can take it to her," Corine insisted. "I'd like to ask her one more thing. She's such an amazing person with so much to give."

"She's pretty wiped out after everything that's happened," I said, wincing. It probably wasn't my place to screen Ginny's fans, but I couldn't help it.

Ginny had been through so much, and the last thing she needed was another eager fan taking up more of her time.

Corine sighed. "You're right. She must be exhausted." She handed over the jacket with a small smile. "It was nice meeting you."

"Likewise. Good night, Corine," I said, hurrying out the door and jogging back to the car.

Within minutes, we were back at the inn. As we walked into the lobby, I couldn't switch off my customer service mode.

"Is there anything I can get for you from the front desk?" I asked Ginny.

"You really are a peach," she said with a tired smile. "But no. I've got Kean if I need anything."

"At least now you can rest until your car is ready. Maybe take a stroll down memory lane and visit some places you knew growing up here," I suggested, not sure what else to say.

Ginny chuckled. "I wish. Kean and I have to go to the high school tomorrow. The same high school I graduated from. Ugh, I was in such a hurry to get out of there as a teenager. Now look at me, heading back to warn the kids about the pitfalls of a writing career." She laughed. "Want to come?"

"I'd love to, but I have to work," I replied with a smile.

"That's right. You've got a job. I forgot. In that case, I'll see you in the morning at breakfast."

I turned and headed to my room, ready to finally slouch and breathe. Changing into pajamas and sinking into bed felt like heaven.

Ginny might not have enjoyed every moment of her chaotic day, but she was living an exciting life. Even with all the hiccups and detours, she made the life of a writer look wonderfully romantic. I fell asleep thinking that... and woke up realizing her career was far more dangerous than anyone would expect.

Chapter 7

I was at the front desk at my usual time, just a little before seven o'clock. Stella had already replaced yesterday's flowers with a fresh bouquet that filled the lobby with a soft, sweet scent. A few guests appeared in workout gear or pajamas, heading to breakfast. As I reviewed the day's check-ins and check-outs, I noticed Kean strolling the grounds outside, a steaming cup of coffee in hand.

He didn't see me as he headed out the front door, and for a moment, I considered following him. I'd been feeling brave enough to ask him about his relationship with Ginny. Was he just a paid employee, or was there something more between them? The idea that their connection was purely professional felt anticlimactic. But before I could make up my mind, work distracted me, as it always did.

That distraction explained why I didn't notice Kean come back in through the lobby doors. I didn't see him staggering until he tripped across the beautiful Persian rug, almost directly in front of the desk. And I certainly didn't notice the blood until he pulled his hand away from the back of his head.

"Kean! Are you all right?" I gasped, rushing around the desk to help him into one of the soft lobby chairs.

"I think so," he muttered, glancing at his hand now smeared with blood.

"I'll call an ambulance," I said, reaching for the phone.

He grabbed my hand, stopping me. "I don't need an ambulance," he grumbled, his tone unmistakably stubborn. "Just call Gin. I'll be fine."

I straightened, still holding his hand, and placed my other hand on my hip. "No. I'm calling an ambulance. You don't have to go with them, but they're coming to check you out. You might need stitches."

"I think the bleeding is stopping," he argued.

"I'll lose my job if I don't call 9-1-1," I countered firmly.

Kean looked up at me and, with a reluctant nod and an exaggerated eye roll, conceded. I quickly dialed the number, relaying the situation to the dispatcher. Once I'd hung up, I called Ginny's room. I wasn't sure she even hung up before she came flying down the stairs, her face a mix of worry and anger.

"Kean, what happened?" Ginny demanded, kneeling beside him and taking his hand in hers. "I should have told you to sit this one out. It was David, wasn't it? He's gone off the deep end."

"I don't know who it was," Kean replied, his voice low. "My back was turned. Someone snuck up on me while I was in the car looking for my sunglasses." He reached gingerly toward the back of his head, wincing slightly. Thankfully, the bleeding had already begun to slow.

"You're going to the hospital," Ginny said firmly, her grip on his hand tightening.

"You know me better than that, Gin," Kean said, his tone carrying a hint of exasperation.

"The police are going to want to talk to you," she pressed. I nodded in agreement.

"Then they can come here," Kean snapped. "I'm not going to any hospital or police station."

"You are the most stubborn man," Ginny hissed through clenched teeth.

"And you worry too much," he shot back.

"Did they take your wallet?" I asked, the thought suddenly crossing my mind.

Without letting go of Ginny's hand, Kean patted his pockets and pulled out a black leather wallet. He handed it to Ginny, who flipped it open and froze.

"Yikes," she said, her expression tightening.

"What is it?" I asked, stepping closer.

"All your money is still here. You've got this much? What are you doing walking around with all this on you?" Ginny asked, holding up the wallet with a bemused expression.

"How much is there?" Kean asked.

"Almost three hundred in cash. Not to mention the credit cards and… nice. I don't think I've ever seen your driver's license picture. You look like you should be on a Wanted poster," she teased, managing to coax a small smile from him.

The EMTs arrived quickly, their efficiency cutting through the tension. Stella joined the small group gathered around Kean, her presence calm and reassuring. Max, however, remained conspicuously absent. That struck me as odd. Max was usually on top of anything happening at the inn, and something this serious, a guest being attacked on the property, should have had him front and center. If he thought having the Wildflower Inn mentioned in a steamy romance novel was bad for business, an assault in the parking lot would surely top his list of concerns.

The first EMT dropped his orange tackle box on the floor, flipping it open to retrieve a penlight. Standing behind Kean, he shined the light on the wound. "This isn't a deep cut," he said. "But you're going to have a goose egg. The bruising's already started. At any point, were you unconscious?"

Kean exhaled deeply. "I walked outside, looking at my phone. Went up to the car to grab my sunglasses. I leaned in, found them, and was about to slam the door shut when I got walloped. Dropped to my knees, saw stars and Tweety birds. Managed to get up and make it to the lobby."

He winced as he reached for the lump on his head, his expression pained but stoic.

"You should probably go to the emergency room," the EMT said. "You might have a concussion."

"Nope," Kean replied firmly.

"Kean, you need to be checked," Ginny interjected, gripping his hand tightly. "I can't have anything happen to that beautiful head of yours."

"Gin, I can't leave you alone to…"

"Right, because I'm not capable of taking care of myself," she snapped, glaring at him.

"You remember what happened last time. And don't tell me there's no possibility that I leave for a couple of hours and come back to find you married to husband number five," Kean countered dryly.

Ginny stared at him with a straight face. "Very funny. Take him away, boys. Give him a thorough colonoscopy while you're at it."

Kean chuckled but winced again as the EMTs packed up their equipment.

"We'll grab the stretcher and…"

"Nope. No stretcher. I'll walk," Kean said, standing slowly and pressing a white bandage to the cut on his head.

"Really?" Ginny muttered. "You just have to be the macho man, don't you? Can't let them wheel you out of here. Gotta walk like you're John Wayne or something."

"If I were John Wayne, you'd be the ornery woman who got a pop in the chops," Kean grumbled. "Something I should have done years ago."

"I'd love to see you try, old man. I'll meet you at the hospital," Ginny shot back, crossing her arms.

There wasn't an easy solution to this. With four incidents now surrounding Ginny—David, Pete, the vandalism, and this attack—Kean was headed to the hospital, leaving her vulnerable. The thought tied my stomach in knots.

"What should we do?" I whispered to Stella, who had been quietly observing the scene.

"I'll ask Max," she replied, her expression unreadable as she turned toward his office.

With Ginny, Kean, and the paramedics gone, the lobby slowly returned to its usual rhythm. Guests milled about, enjoying their vacations, blissfully unaware of the tension that lingered. But I couldn't shake the worry gnawing at me. As it turned out, I wasn't the only one.

Chapter 8

About fifteen minutes before my shift ended, a familiar face appeared in the lobby. It was Corine Schofield. She had a suitcase in one hand and a duffle bag in the other.

"I was wondering if I'd run into you," Corine said with a smile as she made her way to the front desk.

"What are you doing here?" I asked, genuinely surprised.

"I got a room! Turns out a little diligence pays off. I'd been hoping for a cancellation or an early check-out, and it worked. I won't lie—it's because Geneva Panchella is staying here. I'm hoping for a chance to pick her brain a little more. You don't think she'll mind, do you?" Corine asked eagerly.

"She seems very gracious with her fans," I replied diplomatically. "But with everything that's been going on, I can't say what kind of mood she might be in." I hesitated, then added, "Not that I'm an expert. I've never even read one of her stories. At least not yet." I held up my copy of Ginny's latest book, which I'd brought to the desk in case I had any downtime.

"Is she in the hotel now?" Corine asked, her eyes bright with hope.

"No, she left a little while ago. I'm not sure when she'll be back." I avoided mentioning Kean's attack or that Ginny had gone to the emergency room with him. It wasn't my place to share that kind of information, and Max wouldn't appreciate me spreading any details that could alarm guests.

"I felt so terrible about her car. It sure was pretty," Corine said sympathetically.

"Were you still at the book signing when that happened?"

"No, I read about it in the local paper. It made the news because she's from Sierra Hills. The article said she'd be staying in town until her car was fixed," Corine replied.

"Wow. That reporter really got the scoop," I muttered as I finished checking Corine into her room. She was on the second floor, at the opposite end of the inn from Ginny's room. I handed her the plastic key card and gave her the usual information about kitchen hours. "Enjoy your stay," I said with a smile.

"Thank you. I'm sure I'll be seeing you around," she replied, slinging her duffle bag over her shoulder and lifting her suitcase with her free hand.

I nodded politely as she headed down the hall toward the rooms. I didn't mention that her room was just one door away from mine. Corine seemed sweet, but Ginny's growing list of admirers was starting to make me concerned.

As I stood at the desk, a sudden wave of unease washed over me, as if someone were watching me. I scanned the lobby. There weren't any suspicious shadows anywhere. Then, out of the corner of my eye, I thought I saw a man in a cowboy hat quickly duck out of sight near the window.

Could it be Pete with the belt buckle trophy? Could he be waiting for Ginny, knowing she went to the hospital with Kean? My pulse quickened.

"Calm yourself, Sophie," I muttered under my breath. "You can't even be sure you saw a man in a cowboy hat, let alone know it was Pete. You're letting all this drama get to you."

Just then, I felt a hand on my shoulder. Startled, I let out an ear-piercing yelp and spun around, only to find Max standing behind me, his eyes wide and his hand pressed to his chest.

"What? What is it?" he barked, clearly as startled as I was.

I let out a long groan. "You scared me to death."

"I scared you? I'm surprised the mirrors on the walls didn't shatter with that scream," Max said, his expression an amusing mix of annoyance and amusement.

"Scream? Was I really that loud?"

"Wait. Let me listen."

"For what?"

"For the dogs to start howling. That shriek of yours could've been mistaken for a dog whistle," he teased, smirking.

"Very funny. Don't sneak up on people," I said, trying to keep my tone serious.

"So, is Miss Panchella back?" he asked, shifting topics.

"You heard about her going to the hospital? You

aren't going to throw her out, are you?" I asked, narrowing my eyes.

"You sound like my mother," Max replied with a sigh.

"Well, are you?" I pressed.

Max took a deep breath. "No. Not because I don't want to, but because all the other hotels, motels, and rooms for rent are booked solid. I wouldn't have anywhere to transfer her. If I were to tell her to leave without cause, we'd be wide open to a lawsuit. It isn't worth it. But I'm standing firm on her not using the inn in her next novel. I'll make it clear we'll sue if she decides to use the Wildflower Inn or any likeness of it."

"Have you talked to her about how you feel? Instead of leading with lawyers, maybe you could come to an agreement," I suggested cautiously.

"I've made up my mind," Max replied firmly. "We've worked too hard to make the Wildflower a simple, welcoming place with beautiful rooms and good wine. I won't see it turned into a no-tell motel in some sleazy novel that millions of people will read about. What kind of weirdos do you think that'll attract?"

I bit my tongue. *We might already be too late*, I

thought as Max turned and strode back to his office.

Needing a break, I decided to get some fresh air before heading to my room. One of the perks of working at the Wildflower was its beautiful grounds, and the vineyard was my favorite spot. As soon as the sun hit my face, the tension in my shoulders eased. The crisp air carried the earthy scent of freshly cut grass and rich soil, making it easy to forget the bustling little town just outside the gates. Looking down the neat rows of vines supported by wooden stakes and twine, I could only hear the distant chirping of birds. Or so I thought.

A voice broke through the calm, loud and agitated. I scanned the rows of vines and spotted a few vineyard hands moving methodically through the foliage, seemingly undisturbed. Finally, I zeroed in on the direction of the raised voice. It didn't take long to realize it was Lucinda.

Lucinda Foreman, the vineyard manager, was talking with one of her vineyard hands. Her voice, usually calm and measured, had an edge to it. From what I'd observed over the past few weeks, Lucinda was as much a part of the vineyard as the vines themselves. She'd been here for over thirty years, and I wouldn't have been surprised if she had names for each plant.

"I don't like it," she huffed. "I'm going to have to talk to Stella and Max about this. I just can't have it."

Curiosity got the better of me. I walked over, giving a quick wave and hunching my shoulders slightly. "Hi. I hope I'm not interrupting."

"No, Sophie, not at all," Lucinda said, her tone softening as she dismissed the young man beside her. "Make sure that incident report has all the details you just told me," she instructed. The vineyard hand nodded and hurried toward her office.

"Incident report?" I asked, my curiosity piqued. "What happened?"

"We had someone running through the vineyard earlier," Lucinda explained, her lips pinching together in frustration. "The intern just told me now because we had two tours come through, and we're short-staffed again this year for the harvest. I'm supposed to have three more people joining the crew next week. I can't have anyone running through my vineyard."

Her wide-brimmed sunhat shaded her face, but I could see the fire in her eyes. She was protective of this place, and I couldn't blame her.

"Did they see what the person looked like?" I asked. I didn't want to jump to conclusions, but with everything that had been happening lately, I couldn't ignore how odd this sounded. Coincidences weren't something I believed in, and this felt like one more piece of a troubling puzzle.

"Whoever it was wore a cowboy hat and jeans," Lucinda said. Her words hit me like a jolt, and before I could stop myself, my hand shot up to my mouth and my eyes widened. So much for being discreet.

"What? Does that mean something to you?" she asked, her brow furrowed.

I took a deep breath. "One of our guests has been having some trouble with… stalkers."

"Stalkers? Plural?" Lucinda repeated, her tone sharpening.

"It looks that way. She has a knack for rubbing people the wrong way." I hated to talk about Ginny like that, but it wasn't untrue. Belt Buckle Pete's critique meltdown revealed him to be just as volatile as Ginny's ex.

Of course, I couldn't entirely judge. Ansel had stalked me so badly that I'd had to leave the city. Thinking back, I couldn't pinpoint what I'd done to make him feel the need to control me. But maybe it didn't matter. Whether it was me, a girl at a coffee shop, or a jogger on the sidewalk, he'd been determined to dominate anyone who let him. It wasn't about who—just what he could get away with.

"That's awful," Lucinda said, shaking her head. "Well, I can tell you one thing. If it turns out to be one of her stalkers, they're going to regret stepping foot in my vineyard."

"I wouldn't want to be them," I said with a small smile and a shake of my head.

"Did you say you were short-staffed? Is there anything I can do to help? I'm still staying on the property since I haven't found an apartment yet. I might be able to give you a few hours a week," I offered. It was true. My apartment search was dragging, and I often found myself itching for something to do in the afternoons, something outdoors that could stretch both my muscles and my mind.

"Really, Sophie? That would be great. I promise not to work you too hard," Lucinda said with a warm smile. Even with dirt smudging her jeans and her floral-printed rain boots, she had an elegance about her, like the matriarch of a sprawling estate in a Regency romance novel. She was tough, but it was the kind of toughness that came from decades of experience running the vineyard. It didn't take away from her grace.

"I'd be thrilled to help," I replied. Not only would it give me fresh air and exercise, but it would also let me keep an eye on the inn and watch for any suspicious characters. "Maybe having more people out in the rows will be enough to deter trespassers."

"I don't understand it," Lucinda said with a huff. "We have signs up, and who in their right mind wants to go through the wire fences? Not to mention the ground's a mess with dry patches and mud. On the other side of the vineyard, it's two miles of wide-open space and then the mall. What makes someone think traipsing through my grapes is the best route?"

"I'm sorry," I offered, unsure of what else to say. There was no way I'd start speculating about Pete just because the trespasser wore a cowboy hat. But if someone was determined enough to bash Kean on the head and bolt through the vineyard, I doubted they were done causing trouble.

"Don't you worry," Lucinda said with a wink. "If they come back, I'll catch them. Remind me to tell you the story sometime about how I keep our grounds so pristine." She tilted her head toward me.

"You have any kick-around clothes you don't mind getting dirty?"

"I do," I replied.

"Then is there any reason to wait until tomorrow?" she asked.

"Nope," I said with a grin. I went to change and returned to the vineyard, eager to help and curious about what I might find. Lucinda had mentioned the trespasser ran off toward the far end of the vineyard, so I made my way in that direction. I didn't expect to find anything. But I did. Boy, did I.

Chapter 9

Thankfully, I started in the vineyard at four in the afternoon. By six, when everyone was calling it a day, I was thoroughly exhausted. How out of shape had I become that a couple of hours picking grapes left me ready to collapse? It was embarrassing. Still, I couldn't resist checking the area Lucinda mentioned, where the trespasser was spotted earlier.

The logical thing to look for was footprints. I expected to find cowboy boot prints but didn't see anything resembling them. Instead, I found a few gym shoe tracks, most likely left by the vineyard hands as they moved up and down the rows. Just as I was about to give up, something caught my eye, a piece of paper stuck to the base of a vine bursting with purple grapes.

At first, I assumed it was a grocery list or directions to some other spot in town. But as I bent down and picked it up, I realized it wasn't ordinary paper. It was a page from a book. The top of the page read *The Red Tropic Lily*, and the bottom was marked with the page number 132. It was from Ginny's latest book—the one she'd been signing at the bookstore, the one she'd given me a copy of. My stomach tightened. This was a strange coincidence for someone who didn't believe in coincidences.

"What do I do with this?" I muttered under my breath. Even if the page carried fingerprints that matched Pete or David, it wouldn't prove much. It was just a page from Ginny's book. There was no blood, no cryptic confession scrawled in the margins. It didn't scream "clue" in any obvious way. Sighing, I folded the paper and stuffed it into my pocket before heading back to the inn to wash up and grab something to eat.

Though I hadn't cracked the case or uncovered anything groundbreaking, I felt a sense of accomplishment. The afternoon had given me a comfortable fatigue, both physically from the vineyard work and mentally from puzzling over the mystery.

My shower felt heavenly, and slipping into a fresh set of comfy clothes gave me a second wind. By seven o'clock, I looked like any other guest winding down for the night. I headed downstairs, planning to order something to eat and bring it back to my room. But before I could make it to the restaurant in the basement, I was ambushed.

"Sophie!"

I paused at the top of the stairs as my stomach growled in protest. Turning, I spotted Ginny with Corine at her side. Corine smiled brightly and waved, while Ginny planted her hands on her hips in a way that made me feel like I was about to get scolded.

"Hello, ladies," I said cautiously. "Ginny, how's Kean?"

Inwardly, I wracked my brain, wondering if I'd done something to upset Ginny. But it wasn't me she was annoyed with. It was someone else entirely.

"I just got through tucking him in for the night," Ginny replied, her tone lightening slightly. "He was released. No concussion, thankfully, but he did need stitches. I've always said he had a hard head." Her wry comment made both Corine and me chuckle.

"I'm glad to hear that," I said sincerely. "But

you seem upset. Is something wrong with the inn? Anything I can help with?"

Ginny's expression darkened. "Sierra Hills' constable, Detective Connor, could use a couple of lessons in manners," she hissed.

I glanced at Corine, who offered a sheepish smile and a shrug. "Apparently, he wasn't much help at the hospital," she said.

I raised an eyebrow, intrigued but not entirely surprised. Detective Connor didn't strike me as someone who prioritized bedside manner.

"Wasn't much help? He wasn't any help at all," Ginny huffed. "He said Pete Larson was a staple in the community and that his wife bakes pies for all the town fairs. Sierra Hills hasn't changed since I was a kid. Certain people cover for certain other people. It's not what you know but who. I'm not saying they should shackle the guy and bury him under the jail, but at least go talk to him! If Pete has an alibi, then fine, hunt down my ex-husband. It's one of those two crazies making this trip down memory lane an absolute fiasco." She placed a dramatic hand on her fore-head. For a moment, I wondered if part of her was relishing the chaos as potential fodder for her next novel.

"You just need to be patient," Corine said gently. I nodded in agreement.

Ginny took a deep breath and smirked. "The wheels of justice move slow. Slower still in a small town where resources are limited and the cries of the small-town girl who made it big aren't taken as seriously as someone who's lived here for fifty years."

"Corine's right," I added. "I've talked to Detective Connor before. He might seem aloof, but I think there's a lot going on in his head."

"Yeah, if you want to call his marbles rolling around 'a lot going on,'" Ginny quipped, making Corine and me laugh. "I haven't had a thing to eat all day. Would you ladies care to join me?"

"I'd love to," Corine began, "but I'd really like to dive into the notes you gave me. Miss Panchella, I can't thank you enough for your pointers. I hope I wasn't too forward in asking for your help. It's just… I'm a little intimidated by someone with your level of talent."

"Oh, posh," Ginny said, waving her hand dismissively.

"It's true," Corine insisted. "But I've taken up enough of your time. Like I said, if you need anything, I'm just down the hallway. Feel free to impose." She smiled broadly and gave a cheerful wave as she walked away.

I let out a deep breath, rubbing my stomach absentmindedly. "I was just about to sneak down to the restaurant and ask the chef if he could whip me up something simple. Would you…"

Ginny put up her hand, stopping me mid-sentence. Her authoritative gesture reminded me of Superman halting a speeding train. Once again, I thought I was in trouble.

"You have been such a dear," Ginny said. "I'm taking you to dinner. I've got a taste for Italian. Do you know of any good Italian restaurants in town? The last time I was here, when I was eighteen, the closest thing Sierra Hills had was a Domino's Pizza. And I don't need to tell you that's anything but Italian." She rolled her eyes.

"I do know of a place, but I'm really not dressed for it, and…"

"Nonsense," Ginny interrupted. "A woman with your figure and naturally thick hair doesn't need to dress up. You look beautiful. Now, come on. Tell me where this place is."

Before I could protest, Ginny linked her arm through mine and pulled me toward the door. There was no saying no. Resigning myself to my fate, I flipped my hair over my shoulder and let her lead the way. I looked more like I was headed to the gym than out to dinner, but Ginny's charm made it impossible to argue. We walked to the mechanic's loaner car, Ginny chatting all the while.

In minutes, we were parked in front of La Bella Vita. I learned just how much Ginny and I had in common. The thought sent a shiver down my spine. I couldn't help it. The realization frightened me.

Chapter 10

It was impossible for Ginny not to make an entrance. Over the past couple of days, I'd grown accustomed to the flamboyant author showing up dressed like the mistress at a famous mobster's funeral. Tonight was no different. As soon as we walked into the restaurant, all eyes turned to her. Especially Mariana, the owner of the place. A classic Italian beauty, Mariana was the polar opposite of her younger sister, Simona, who managed housekeeping at the inn. While Simona and I got along famously, Mariana... well, she wasn't unfriendly, but there was a coolness to her. At least toward me. When her eyes flicked up from the bar, where I noticed another familiar face, I could feel the heat of her gaze. She moved toward the hostess station like a snake slinking across sand.

"Buona sera," Mariana greeted us, raising one perfectly arched eyebrow as she looked both of us up and down. "Sophie, good to see you again."

"Hi, Mariana. This is…"

"Geneva Panchella," Ginny interrupted, her chin lifted imperiously, her eyes hooded. "I'm staying at the inn. Would you happen to have a quiet table for two, away from the kitchen, preferably with a window? And please bring a bottle of your house red wine to the table."

"Oh, uh, yes. Of course," Mariana stammered, pulling two menus from the stack before leading us to a table that perfectly fit Ginny's description.

As soon as Ginny sat down, she took a deep breath. I followed her gaze to the window and realized she was watching the car parked outside. It was clear that was on her mind when she requested a window seat.

Mariana handed us our menus and assured us a waiter would be along shortly.

"Don't forget the wine," Ginny added without looking up.

I sat down cautiously, glancing at Mariana's retreating figure. To my surprise, she seemed slightly rattled by Ginny's abruptness. I didn't think anything could shake Mariana. She always struck me as someone who exuded composure but had the quiet intensity to send someone a dead fish in the mail if they crossed her. Or maybe I'd just seen too many movies.

Once the wine was poured, Ginny lifted her glass. "To life," she toasted. I picked up my glass and clinked it with hers before taking a sip.

"This wine is delicious," she said, swirling the glass in her hand.

"It should be. It's from our vineyard," I replied proudly. For a few minutes, I held the floor, telling Ginny about working in the rows harvesting grapes until the new staff arrived next week. The sense of accomplishment warmed me almost as much as the wine.

"You're a real puzzle," Ginny said after taking another sip, her eyes narrowing thoughtfully.

"You think?" I asked, wrinkling my nose.

"What brought you to Sierra Hills? You're not a local. You don't fit in. Anyone from here can tell that just by looking at you. What's your story?"

I shrugged, considering how much to say. But something about Ginny made me feel safe enough to open up. Maybe it was the fact that we shared one terrible, scary thing in common. Taking a deep breath, I spilled the beans about Ansel, my ex-boyfriend turned stalker, the man who made me leave the city and start over in Sierra Hills.

The thing that surprised me most was how Ginny asked questions. I'd known her for a total of three days, each one marked by a catastrophe more upsetting than the last, and yet I found her charming. She could have easily sat across from me, venting about her own misfortunes, but instead, she focused on me.

"Does he know where you are?" Ginny asked, her gaze steady.

"No. At least I don't think he does. What I don't understand is, if I was such an obstacle to his happiness and success, why did he want to keep me around? Why did he want me to come back? You'd think if I was such an embarrassment, he'd be glad I was gone," I huffed, tearing off a piece of breadstick.

"It isn't about that," Ginny said firmly. "He was telling you exactly how he really sees himself. He sees himself as an embarrassment, an unhappy person. It's a heck of a lot easier for someone like that to say it's you rather than look in the mirror and say it's me. So, he's going to try to convince you the world is a dangerous place without him, even if he has to make it dangerous himself. You already know this. He cared more about himself than he ever cared about you."

Her words hit me like a cold slap. They were blunt and painful but undeniably true. I'd already reconciled the fact that I'd never go back to Ansel, not for my safety and certainly not for my sanity. Still, hearing Ginny lay it out so plainly stirred something in me. My love for Ansel had been real —at least, I'd thought it was. But now, the pang I felt wasn't for him. It was for the realization that his love for me had never been what I thought it was.

Thankfully, our food arrived, breaking the intensity of the moment. I had penne with meatballs and arrabbiata sauce, while Ginny's choice was chicken vesuvio. Each bite of my meal tasted better than the last, and I was grateful when Ginny began talking about herself, giving me a chance to focus on eating.

"I should have stopped at three husbands," she said, shaking her head as she took a bite of her food. "David has been the biggest mistake of them all. A loose cannon." She rolled her eyes and dabbed her lips with a napkin, the contented look on her face suggesting the meal was at least helping to soothe her frustration. "There's nothing like Italian comfort food."

"But you loved him when you married him?" I asked, curious.

"I loved all my husbands. The first one was the best. He died just before my first book came out. That book was based on our relationship... loosely," she added with a wink. "My second husband was a good man. But we both married for the wrong reasons. We were lonely and thought we'd grow together. Instead, we grew apart. No hard feelings when we went our separate ways. Thankfully, he was much wealthier than me and offered a very generous divorce settlement."

She paused to take another bite, then continued. "I swung in the opposite direction for my third husband, mistaking boring for stable. And then... the pièce de résistance: David. That was the biggest mistake of all. It would be one thing if I were the only one who had to deal with him, but as you can see, he's seeped into everything, like septic water in a basement. And he smells just as bad."

"Why did you get divorced?" I asked, genuinely curious about what had driven her to finally walk away.

"David thought himself quite the poet, especially after a few shots of Jack," Ginny said, her tone dripping with disdain. "Yes, he took great pride in rhyming. Mediocrity at best. But when you're a wife, you encourage. You gently instruct or nudge—never scold or criticize. That's what I thought marriage was about. I'd been in three so far and was happy to praise my men for their accomplishments. My first husband installed a new toilet in our house. You praise that kind of thing.

"But some people will beat the praise out of you if they have to—and they don't need fists to do it. That was David. A textbook narcissist."

It wasn't surprising to me anymore how Ginny came to be a romance writer. I'd bet she was always looking for love, like the song says, in all the wrong places. But in her books, she could create beautifully flawed characters, finding each other in spontaneous, perfect ways. Her characters could be happy even if she wasn't.

That was probably why the next words ran out of my mouth before I could stop them.

"What about Kean?"

Ginny's lips curled into a smirk as she arched her right eyebrow. "You think there's something going on between us?"

"I don't know," I said quickly. "I'm not trying to

pry. It's just… he seems very protective of you. I'd also wonder what a husband might think of a man like him being around you all the time."

I hoped I hadn't offended her, but Ginny took it in stride.

"Kean has been with me so long I can't remember a time without him. The truth is… well, maybe I'll just keep you guessing. Half my success comes from letting my readers draw their own conclusions," she said with a sly smile. Her confidence was contagious, and I couldn't help but smile back.

"You aren't afraid of David?" I asked.

Ginny turned her gaze to the window, her eyes narrowing slightly as she looked at the loaner car. "I wasn't, until he tried to drive us off the road when we first arrived. That's when I realized he'd lost some of his marbles. But what he did to my car, to Kean… it's unacceptable."

When the check arrived, Ginny snatched it up before I could even offer to treat. Then, with a whistle loud enough to turn every head in the restaurant, she called out to Mariana.

"Honey, can I get a plate of mostaccioli with meat sauce and sausage to go? Ring it up separately. Thanks, toots," she said cheerfully, earning chuckles and eye-rolls from some of the patrons. Her name was whispered at a few tables, the familiar hum of recognition following her.

As we left the restaurant, Jesse hopped up from the bar and hurried to hold the door for us. His charming smile lit up his face as I introduced him to Ginny.

"You two looked like you were having a good time," he said, his blue eyes twinkling. "I'm glad there wasn't a problem with what Max said."

I froze. "What do you mean?" Ginny asked, her tone cool but sharp.

"About not using the inn as the setting for your next novel," Jesse said hesitantly, his gaze darting between Ginny and me as his smile faltered.

Ginny's expression hardened. "Mr. Amandes didn't say anything of the sort. Is there some kind of problem?"

This wasn't a crazy ex-lover or a disgruntled amateur writer. This was someone telling her what she could and couldn't write about. By the look on Ginny's face, it was clear to me that no one, not even Max, told Geneva Panchella what she could or couldn't do.

Chapter 11

"All right, you two. Climb in and hold on. We're about to attract some attention," Ginny said, her tone clipped but laced with determination. I did as I was told, sliding into the passenger seat while Jesse climbed into the back. Ginny started the car, revved the engine, and peeled out of the parking lot like the devil was chasing us.

"The speed limit is only thirty, I think," Jesse muttered from the back seat. I clutched the seatbelt strap across my chest, holding on for dear life as cars honked and swerved. Ginny weaved through traffic, rolling through an orange light as if it were a mere suggestion.

When we finally pulled into the inn's parking lot, she slammed on the brakes, got out, and grabbed her carry-out bag. Without missing a beat, she slammed the driver's door shut with such force that I froze in place.

"Is she drunk?" Jesse whispered.

"No," I replied, unbuckling quickly. "She's mad. And I mean angry mad, not crazy mad."

"Then we better get in there," Jesse said, following my lead. Within seconds, we were inside the lobby, where Ginny was banging the silver bell on the front desk with a vengeance. Max emerged from his office, his brows furrowed into a deep scowl.

"Just the guy I wanted to see," Ginny said, her hand planted firmly on her hip. "Would you mind telling me why I can't use the Wildflower Inn in my next novel? I thought we'd discussed this. Stella doesn't have a problem. What's yours?"

Max's gaze swept over her, then shifted to Jesse and me. Despite towering over Ginny, she didn't budge an inch.

"Our mother doesn't run the inn," Max said calmly, though his tone was edged with frustration. "She's semiretired. My brother and I run it now, and I…we…don't think it would be good for business to dredge up the negative incidents from the past and glamorize them."

"You had some counterfeiters and a murder. It's hardly the Jeffrey Dahmer apartment," Ginny huffed, making Jesse and me chuckle—until Max shot us a warning look.

"This is our family's business," Max insisted. "We have a say in the matter. And we say no."

I hated seeing Max like this. It was obvious he was only thinking about what was best for the Wildflower, but I couldn't see how setting a romance novel here could hurt. In fact, it seemed like free publicity to me.

"Funny how everyone in this little town where I grew up is happy to take my money," Ginny shot back, "but the minute I ask for something in return, you all act like you're surviving on tack bread and powdered milk. I'm afraid you can't stop me, Mr. Amandes."

"If we have to, we'll get the courts involved," Max said flatly. His tone was unsettling, and when I glanced at Jesse, his expression mirrored my own shock. Jesse's mouth hung open, his eyebrows pinched together in disbelief. Clearly, neither of us had ever seen Max like this before.

"Do what you have to," Ginny said, her voice icy. "But I'm writing about the Wildflower Inn, and

I'm sparing no details. Maybe I'll even add you in it."

Max's jaw tightened. "Did you ever think that maybe this is why you're plagued with so much bad luck lately? Maybe someone's trying to tell you something. If you don't start listening soon, you're going to find yourself in real trouble."

His words sent a chill through the air. Ginny's fiery demeanor didn't falter, but I couldn't help wondering what had driven Max to say something so ominous.

"Is that so? I'll be sure to let Detective Connor know you're so concerned," Ginny replied, her tone cold as she turned on her heel. After saying good-night to Jesse and me, she took her takeout bag upstairs, leaving a tense silence in her wake.

"Max, what was that all about?" Jesse asked, his voice laced with disbelief.

"I meant every word of it," Max said calmly, his eyes fixed on the computer as he checked the remaining arrivals.

"You can't talk to a guest like that. Do you realize we're sold out because of her?" Jesse said, his tone sharp with condemnation. I took a step back, keeping out of the line of fire. After all, I just worked here.

"She's been nothing but trouble since she arrived," Max snapped.

"But you don't see anyone leaving because of her. On the contrary, at La Bella Vita I overheard people recognizing her. She's got a seminar tomorrow at the high school, and it's going to be packed. Having a famous writer stay here is good for business, Max. Letting her write about the Wild-flower would be even better. Why can't you see that?"

Max didn't even look up. "If you made the right decisions, you'd be in charge. But you're not. I am."

Jesse's jaw tightened. "I'm not stupid, Max. Mom thinks it's a good idea. I think it's a good idea. Half the staff think it's a good idea for her to write about the inn. Sophie has been chatting with Geneva since she arrived. Isn't that right?" He turned to me, and my cheeks heated up. I didn't want to pick sides. I could see where both men were coming from, but getting in the middle of a family argument seemed like a surefire way to lose my job.

Max lowered his voice and leaned closer to his brother, glancing over his shoulder to ensure no one else was listening. "Jesse, there are things you don't know about this place. It's more than just wine and the criminal activity from the bootlegging days.

People don't want to eat in a place where a dead body was found. They don't want to know a part-time handyman killed someone. How do you think they'll look at us? And I have a feeling that's just the tip of the iceberg."

"What about the place where Lizzie Borden lived? People stay there all the time hoping to see something paranormal. Why do people still photograph the Amityville house?" Jesse countered.

"That was all a hoax," I blurted before I could stop myself. Both Jesse and Max turned to look at me like I'd sprouted a third eye. Realizing I'd interrupted a delicate argument, I clamped my lips shut, regretting my need to chime in.

"Is that what you want the Wildflower to be?" Max continued, ignoring me. "A tacky tourist trap that boasts about its shady past? I don't want that. This place has our name attached to it. It should feel like a home away from home, not a carnival funhouse." His voice grew angrier with every word.

"Geneva doesn't write trashy pulp. She writes good stories," Jesse said, his voice low but firm. "If you ever bothered to read one, you'd know that. But that would mean admitting you might be wrong."

"The only thing I was wrong about was giving you a job here."

"If you want me to quit, Max, just say so!" Jesse fired back, his frustration bubbling over.

"The idea is sounding better and better," Max said, glaring at his brother.

"Okay," I interjected, unable to stay quiet any longer. This was getting out of hand. "I know I'm not part of the family, but if I worked with my brother, the last thing I'd want is to say something I couldn't take back and then have to look him in the eye every day."

Whether they took my words to heart or were just annoyed I'd stepped into their business, I couldn't tell. Within seconds, Max turned on his heel and stormed back to his office. Jesse gave me a quick pat on the shoulder and left the inn.

I stood there, feeling awful. Somehow, my liking Ginny and appreciating her work felt wrong in the middle of all this drama. It was easy for me to say, "Let her write the book about the inn." My name wasn't attached to it. But this was where I worked and lived for the time being. The Amandes family had been kind to me, and picking a side felt like betraying them all. Now, I'd inserted myself into a family squabble that was none of my business.

As I stood in the quiet lobby, my mind drifted to Ansel. I longed for the version of him from before he became possessive and scary. Back when he was still funny and kind, when he really wanted to hear my thoughts and ideas. If I still had that Ansel, I'd have told him everything that had just happened. We'd have flipped through Ginny's book together, and I'd have asked what he thought I should do, if anything. But that Ansel didn't exist anymore. I didn't have anyone to turn to.

The exhaustion from the evening—the delicious dinner, the heated argument—suddenly caught up with me. Past my bedtime, I walked to my room, longing for the solitude of my space. Once inside, I locked the door, drew the curtains, and collapsed onto the bed. Ginny's book was on the nightstand. I picked it up and began to read.

I expected to get through a few pages before nodding off. Romance novels weren't my thing, and I'd never had much patience for mushy stories. Or so I thought. But Ginny's book turned out to be so much more than the seedy love triangle I'd expected. Her writing was sharp, her characters compelling. By the time the clock struck one, I was halfway through the novel and completely hooked.

Jesse was right. Featuring The Wildflower Inn in a Geneva Panchella novel would be a fantastic opportunity. If Max took the time to read one of her books, he'd see that they weren't the trashy pulp stories he assumed they were. They were thoughtful and exciting, crafted by a true talent. To be part of a Geneva Panchella story wouldn't tarnish the inn's reputation. It would be a feather in its cap.

But if I thought this little family squabble was rough, I was in for a rude awakening the next day. With every sunrise, I'm reminded: fact is always stranger than fiction.

Chapter 12

The next day, I found myself annoyed that I couldn't continue Ginny's book at the front desk. I was desperate to know what happened next, but reading on the job wasn't exactly professional. It was frustrating, but I knew I'd have to wait.

With the inn at full capacity, most guests here for Ginny's final event, I didn't have much to do. There were no check-outs, and the rooms were only being freshened up. Stella's freshly picked bouquets were already displayed throughout the lobby. My responsibilities boiled down to standing at the desk and answering the occasional question. Breakfast ended at eleven-thirty, free maps of Sierra Hills were available at the entrance, and Geneva

Panchella's event was scheduled from four to six at the high school. That was it. I leaned on the desk, trying not to look as bored as I felt.

Around noon, Ginny swept into the lobby, looking incredible in a purple dress with matching heels. Kean walked proudly behind her, the bandage on the back of his head a stark reminder of the recent drama. I smiled, but Ginny barely acknowledged it before hurrying over to me.

"Do you have a minute?" she whispered.

"Uh, sure. How's Kean feeling?"

"I can hear you, and I'm fine," Kean said, his voice gruff. "Although my mother hen thinks I need to be cocooned in bubble wrap." He rolled his eyes, his expression devoid of humor.

"Pipe down, you," Ginny shot back. "Don't listen to him. He's had a head injury."

"I'll get us a table," Kean huffed, heading toward the dining room for breakfast.

"What can I do for you, Ginny?" I asked, offering a smile.

Ginny took a deep breath, glancing over her shoulder before pulling an envelope from her clutch purse. "This was under my door this morning," she said quietly.

The envelope bore the Wildflower Inn logo. I

opened it, my stomach twisting as I pulled out a sheet of Wildflower Inn stationery, the kind provided in every room for notes or doodles. But this wasn't a harmless doodle. Words, cut from a book, were glued to the page in a way that sent a chill down my spine. The message was cruel, threatening, and deeply unsettling. Just holding the paper, knowing it had been in the hands of someone capable of constructing such a message, made my skin crawl. I wanted to crumple it up and burn it.

"Ginny, did you tell Kean?" I asked, my voice low.

"No," she replied flatly. She narrowed her eyes and shook her head.

"You don't think that Pete guy could've done this?"

"This is from my book," Ginny interrupted. "These words were torn from my last novel. Do you know how I know?" She held up the page, pointing at specific letters. "Because of this font. It looks like your typical book font, but it's not. There's a subtle difference that makes it look cleaner on the page. At least to me it does." She pointed to an "f" and a "y." "See these? They're slightly different from the same letters in the *Sierra Bugle.*" She gestured to the newspaper sitting on the front desk.

Her attention to detail was remarkable, but it only deepened the mystery. Someone had gone to great lengths to deliver this threat, and whoever it was, they weren't done yet.

"Ginny, what do you think this means?" I asked, my voice low.

"I think your boss is trying to scare me. Except he's not all that bright, using the company logo on his threat," she replied with a sigh.

"Max? No. I don't believe it. He's stubborn, maybe a little abrasive, but he doesn't threaten people. I just don't believe it." My stomach sank to my shoes. After everything I'd overheard between Max and Jesse yesterday, could he really stoop to this? My head swirled with doubt, but I couldn't bring myself to tell Ginny about the argument.

"You'll have to give me something more convincing than that," Ginny said, crossing her arms.

"Okay, I'll tell you. Their mother didn't raise them that way," I said, the words tumbling out of my mouth. "You should take a couple of minutes to talk to her. She's around the inn somewhere. I'll send her over to your table. Just, please, don't say anything to Max until you've spoken with Stella. Please?"

Ginny stood there, clearly debating whether to confront Max before or after breakfast. Finally, her expression softened.

"All right. I'll talk to her," she said, taking the threatening letter and slipping it back into her purse. "You're really devoted to this family, aren't you?"

I shrugged. Of course, I was devoted to them. They'd given me a job, a roof over my head, and meals I rarely paid for. I owed them. Ginny turned and sauntered to the dining room, once again drawing the attention of every patron. She was impossible to miss.

I headed to Max's office, where he was sitting at his desk typing on the computer. "I need to leave the front desk for a second," I said.

"Okay," he replied without looking up.

I lingered for a moment, watching him. With his dark features and broad shoulders, Max was undeniably handsome. He wasn't the kind of man who would slip a threatening note under someone's door. That was something a creepy guy with bad gums and a beer gut would do. It had to be David. He'd already tried to run Ginny off the road, vandalized her car, clobbered Kean, and now this. The threats were escalating, getting bolder and more personal.

Lost in thought, I realized I was still standing in the doorway, staring into space as I hashed out this internal debate. Shaking my head, I gave Max a quick wave and set off to find Stella. If anyone could bring some clarity to this chaotic situation, it was her.

Chapter 13

Feeling the sun on my face as soon as I stepped outside instantly lifted my mood. I took a deep breath, savoring the fresh air, and began searching for Stella. My eyes landed on Lucinda, who was chatting with Corine Schofield. I made my way over to them.

"Good morning, Lucinda. Morning, Corine. Lucinda, have you seen Stella anywhere?"

"Hey, Sophie. I think she's in her workshop," Lucinda replied, wiping her brow beneath her sun bonnet. "Will you be working in the vineyard again today? You did a great job yesterday."

"Not today. I'm going to an event at the high school. But you can count on me tomorrow," I said with a smile.

"Are you going to Miss Panchella's talk? I'm going too," Corine added, bouncing on her toes like she had at the book signing when she spoke to Ginny.

"I am," I replied.

"What event is that?" Lucinda asked.

I started to explain that a best-selling romance writer was staying at the inn, but Corine interrupted, her enthusiasm bubbling over like a child announcing Santa Claus was coming.

"She's the greatest writer! I'm not ashamed to say that Geneva Panchella changed my life. Her stories are so uplifting, and her characters are so engrossing. Every time I read one of her books, I come away with a fresh perspective. I know I sound silly, but I don't care."

"You don't sound any sillier than me getting excited about a new method of fermenting or growing grapes. I'm a big ol' nerd," Lucinda replied good-naturedly.

I smiled at Lucinda's attempt to connect, but Corine's face fell slightly, her enthusiasm dimming. I realized Lucinda's comment, though innocent, had stung.

"Uh, I'll be here tomorrow to help with the

harvesting," I said, clearing my throat to break the tension.

"Sounds great," Lucinda said, giving a wave as I tapped Corine on the shoulder and motioned for her to follow me toward Stella's workshop.

"I hope you don't think Lucinda was making fun of you," I said as we strolled. "From what I've seen, she really does live, eat, and breathe this vineyard."

"I know. I've been told I'm a little too sensitive. Most people are just being themselves, and I need to remember that. Not take things so personally," Corine admitted.

"It's okay to be sensitive. What's the alternative? Being insensitive?" I joked with a small chuckle.

"That's true," Corine said, a smile returning to her face. I felt relieved.

"Would you like a ride to the event at the high school?" she asked. "I'm planning to go early to get a good seat. I'd be happy to help."

"I appreciate that, but I've got to work. It'll probably already have started by the time I get there. But thanks anyway."

"No problem, Sophie. Well, I've got a few more things I want to do before my vacation officially ends. I'll keep an eye out for you later," she said with a wave, veering off toward the inn.

Stella's workshop came into view ahead. The charming she-shed was painted white with pink shutters, and wildflowers in constant bloom surrounded it. Flowerpots of varying sizes and colors were scattered along the gravel path leading to the front screen door. I knocked lightly.

"Yes? Hello?" Stella's warm voice called from inside.

"Hi, Stella. It's Sophie. Can I come in?"

"By all means," Stella replied from somewhere in her workshop, though I couldn't see her yet. Stepping over the threshold, I was greeted by the heavenly scent of flowers mingling with the sweet aroma of homemade jams. The front of her shed was a chaotic yet charming array of dried bouquet supplies covering every surface. In the back, where Stella stood, a small kitchenette was bustling with activity—fresh grapes, mason jars both full and empty, and a stove with a couple of pots bubbling away.

"I'm sorry to bother you," I began, feeling a pang of guilt. Coming here to talk about Max felt like a betrayal. Who was I to question whether her eldest son could threaten a guest? Who was I to get involved at all?

"You're no bother," she said warmly, though her hands kept busy with a bouquet. "I've got to get these bouquets ready for a real bridezilla. She decided at the last minute she wants lavender sprigs instead of baby's breath. I have a feeling she'll change her mind at least two more times before the wedding. I ought to tell her I just received an exotic new bloom and stuff her bouquet with poison ivy. I doubt she'd know the difference."

"Stella, you wouldn't," I chuckled.

"No, but it doesn't mean I don't think about it," she replied with a mischievous smile. "So, what brings you to my lair?"

I took a deep breath, treading lightly as if crossing a frozen pond I wasn't sure could hold my weight. "I don't want to start any trouble, but I feel I have to tell you something."

"Sophie, you aren't quitting already, are you?" Stella asked, her expression serious.

"No! My gosh, no. I love my job. I just hope you don't want to fire me after I tell you this," I replied, wrapping my arms around my waist. After another deep breath, I recounted everything—the argument between Max and Jesse, the threatening note Ginny had received, and the escalating tension. When I finished, I was nearly out of breath, standing there waiting for her response.

"Well, that is interesting," Stella began, her voice taking on a hard edge. I braced myself, expecting a stern reprimand. "First," she continued, "let me apologize on behalf of my sons for their terrible behavior. I did not raise them to act that way."

Her words caught me off guard. The air seemed to lighten, and I let out a breath I hadn't realized I was holding.

"Those two boys love each other," she said with a faint smile. "So much so that even when they were young, I'd catch them fighting in the yard like wild dogs. Yipping, swatting, and tumbling all over the ground, only to stop, covered in scratches and bruises, and laugh together. That's just how brothers are. They need to rub each other the wrong way... constantly." She rolled her eyes, and I couldn't help but laugh.

"I swear, Max will disagree with Jesse just because he knows it'll annoy him. But they should keep their domestic squabbles out of the workplace and away from the staff. It's clearly bothered you, and I can't have that," she said, her tone hardening again.

"I'm all right," I assured her. "It's really the issue with Ginny that has me concerned."

"Did Max have it in him to write a threatening letter?" Stella paused, her eyes narrowing thoughtfully. "I can't say I'm one hundred percent sure he wouldn't. Especially if he and Miss Panchella had words like you said."

"Oh, they did, Stella. They definitely did," I said, cringing slightly.

"He's already upset she wants to write about the history of this place, and he's against it. I can see his point. But I think he's wrong."

"I do too," I replied.

Stella squared her shoulders and lifted her chin, her resolve solidifying. She untied her apron and slipped it over her head before laying it carefully on the workbench. "I think it's time my boys and I have a little talk. I might be partially retired from the daily business of the inn, but I'm not retired from being their mother." She patted my hand reassuringly as she walked past me and out of the shed.

Left alone among the flowers, dried bouquets,

and charming doodads, I felt a strong urge to hide here forever. I didn't want to face Max or Jesse again. What had I done?

I lingered for a few more minutes, inching toward the door while taking in the decorations that adorned Stella's she-shed. There were photographs, both black-and-white and color, capturing her family, the grounds, and what I assumed were dear friends. It was clear this was Stella's sanctuary, a place filled with memories and beauty. One photo caught my eye—a younger Max and Jesse, maybe twelve or thirteen years old, with their arms slung around each other and goofy grins on their dirt-smudged faces. Grass stuck out of their hair, and I couldn't help but imagine they'd just finished one of their brotherly wrestling matches before Stella snapped the picture.

There was no use avoiding the inevitable. Channeling the same confidence I'd seen in Stella moments before, I raised my chin, squared my shoulders, and stepped out of the shed to head back to the inn. But with each step, my confidence seemed to slip. By the time I reached the inn, I was practically slinking through the door, ready to face the fallout.

Before I could make it to the hallway and

escape to my room, I heard someone call my name. I turned around and saw Max standing there.

"Can I talk to you in my office?" he asked.

This was worse than I'd imagined. My stomach dropped. Why had I opened my big mouth? Who was I to meddle in their family dynamics? Stella might not fire me, but Max certainly could. I began mentally inventorying everything in my room, estimating how long it would take to pack.

Max stood in front of his office door, motioning for me to step inside and take a seat. Reluctantly, I obeyed. Once I was seated, he shut the door behind him and moved around his desk to sit across from me. My hands folded tightly in my lap, I braced myself for the worst.

"I'm so sorry," he blurted out, catching me completely off guard.

"What?" I stammered.

"I behaved like a caveman—to you, to Miss Panchella, and… to my idiot brother."

"Uh… er…" I stumbled, unsure of how to respond.

"You don't have to say anything," Max continued, adjusting his tie with a sheepish expression. "My mom told me how upset you were. She didn't mince words, as usual."

"I should have come to you. I shouldn't have gone to your mom. It was sneaky. I'm not part of the family, and I had no right…"

"What are you talking about? Of course, you're family. I acted like a complete buffoon in front of you. That's a right reserved for family only," Max said, his expression so serious I couldn't help but giggle.

"One thing, Sophie. You can always come to me if you think I'm acting like a jerk. My ego isn't so big that I think I can't use some help sometimes," he said with a wink.

"Well, now that you mention it…"

"That was quick," he quipped, making me giggle again.

"It's Miss Panchella…"

"I'm going to apologize to her too and maybe offer her a free night or something to sweeten the deal. You were right. I can't talk to any guest that way, no matter how loopy they seem to me," Max said, raising an eyebrow.

"That would be nice. But she got a threatening letter slipped under her door last night. She was afraid it was from you because it was on Wildflower stationery. And… well, you hadn't exactly made her feel welcome the night before."

Max's face hardened. "I didn't do that. I'd never do that. Has her ex-husband been seen around?"

I shrugged. "I don't know."

"I'll speak to her personally. Do you know if she's around?" he asked.

"Last I saw her, she and Kean were headed to the restaurant," I admitted.

"I wonder what that story is," Max mused.

"I asked her, but she didn't give me an answer," I said with a smirk.

Max nodded thoughtfully. We chatted for a few more minutes about work, and he offered another sincere apology. Finally, I stood on shaky legs, thanked him for being so understanding, and turned toward the door.

"Thank you, Sophie," he said as I opened it. Then, just as I was about to leave, he added, "I don't know what it is about you, but when we're working together, I want to do a better job."

"I feel that way too," I replied with a smile before heading out, determined not to embarrass myself further.

Back at the front desk, even the grumpy check-outs complaining about the empty coffee canister couldn't wipe the smile off my face. Each one was greeted with a cheerful "Come see us again!"

Nothing was going to bother me for the rest of the day.

Or so I thought. Then I went to Ginny's talk at the high school. There, I started to wonder if Ginny wasn't the source of some of her own problems. Still, that was no reason for anyone to try to kill her.

Chapter 14

After my shift, I quickly changed clothes and hurried to the high school to catch Ginny's talk. Sierra Hills High School was small. The auditorium seated about 150 people and was packed with upperclassmen, parents, and other town visitors. I learned that the current vice principal, Christine Lyons, had been in Ginny's graduating class.

By the time I found a seat in the nosebleed section, Christine was already on stage introducing Ginny. From her warm tone and familiarity, it was clear they had been good friends. But when Ginny made her way to the center of the stage and stood at the podium, she wasted no time in setting the record straight.

"I'm happy to see so many faces interested in my writing," she began innocently enough. "By applause, how many people here have read any of my books?"

A burst of applause erupted from the front rows, with a few scattered claps from around me. Most of the audience, however, stayed quiet.

"That's okay," Ginny said with a gracious smile. "I've got books for everyone to take home with them. Read it. Scribble in it. Use it to prop up an uneven couch." Her humor earned a ripple of laughter from the crowd.

"Let me give you a little bit of my history," she continued once the audience settled. One thing about Ginny, she wasn't just a great storyteller on the page; she could captivate a room just as easily.

"I don't know if it still is, but my old address used to be considered the poor side of town. That can be hard on a girl. Oh, not so much when you're little, but in high school? It was definitely a topic of conversation among some of my peers. Isn't that right, Christine?" Ginny turned to the right wing of the stage with a teasing smile.

She continued, "Before I came on stage, Christine reminded me of all the old classmates in the audience tonight. If a word was spoken between us during those four agonizing years, I can bet it wasn't a nice one." The audience chuckled nervously.

"Now, I could name names, dates, and times when my rivals said or did things to remind me that I was poor, that I dressed differently, or that my mom cut my hair. But the truth is, if it weren't for those experiences, I don't think I'd be the writer I am today. I don't think I'd be a success at all. I'd be some mediocre wannabe."

The room fell silent. You could have heard a pin drop. Everyone was listening intently, and I scanned the audience to see who might be holding their breath, dreading the possibility of being named.

"What I'm saying is that God's divine plan can take even the worst experiences and turn them into something good," Ginny said, her voice steady. "How many of you here are in high school right now?"

A bunch of hands shot up.

"And how many of you hate it?" she asked with a knowing grin.

Most of the hands stayed up.

"It gets better. High school is not the real world. If you're like me, one of the misfits or oddballs, you've got a gift somewhere. Channel any of that anger or hurt into something beautiful for yourself. No one cares what anyone in high school thinks. Am I wrong, Christine?"

I would have loved to see Christine's expression. But before I could focus on that, my attention was drawn to a figure standing beneath the exit sign to my right. Short, gray-headed, and looking about twelve months pregnant—it was David, Ginny's latest ex-husband. Before I could act, he quietly slipped out the door.

I wasted no time and followed, but by the time I reached the lobby, he was gone. Rather than search for him alone, I decided the best course of action was to notify Kean. He had to be nearby. There was no way he'd let Ginny be far from his sight.

My heart raced as I tried to figure out where to go. How much time was I wasting? There had to be a backstage entrance; every school had one. Just as I considered heading back to the front of the auditorium to climb up on stage, I saw Corine. She was dressed in her usual black yoga pants and gray hoodie, her ever-present duffle bag slung over her shoulder.

I waved, not wanting to yell and disrupt Ginny's talk, but Corine didn't notice me. Still, I felt sure she'd lead me to the backstage entrance, so I followed. When she opened a heavy door and disappeared inside, I hurried after her, relieved to find I was right. However, by the time I stepped through the door, Corine was nowhere in sight.

The backstage area was a maze of narrow hallways and dimly lit rooms, more confusing than the corridors I'd just been navigating. One offshoot led to a row of makeup tables with round bulbs framing the mirrors, like something out of a Broadway dressing room. Another led to what appeared to be an office, probably for the drama instructor. Finally, I stumbled upon the wing that accessed the main stage. Peeking down the length of the stage, I spotted Kean standing on the far side, his tall frame unmistakable.

How was I supposed to get to him? A curtain hung behind Ginny but in front of the backdrop. If I moved carefully, I might be able to scoot behind it without causing a disturbance and make my way to Kean.

Just as I was about to attempt it, my foot caught on something, and I nearly fell. Looking down, I saw Corine's duffle bag tucked behind the curtain. Why would she leave it here?

So no one would steal it, I thought with a hint of sarcasm. Who would want to lug this bulky thing around all the time? Obviously, she'd never heard of a purse. But then something caught my eye. Sticking out of the slightly open zipper was one of the stickers from my goodie bag at Ginny's first signing—a bulldog in a bumblebee costume.

There could be lots of those stickers, I told myself. But before I could stop, I'd unzipped Corine's bag. Inside, I found the signed copy of Ginny's book that had been in my goodie bag.

"That woman stole my goodie bag," I hissed under my breath.

With mounting annoyance, I flipped through the book and found pages torn and words cut out, just like the ones on the threatening note slipped under Ginny's door. I'd bet dollars to donuts each word cut out would fit perfectly into the blank spaces in this novel. My stomach churned when I noticed page 132 was missing, the same page I'd found in the vineyard. Corine had been the one running through the rows of grapes. Not Pete Larson. Not David. But David was here, at this event. Could he and Corine be working together? The thought made my head spin.

All I knew was that I needed to find Kean. He'd know what to do. After a quick glance over my shoulder to make sure I was still alone, I dug deeper into the bag. Inside were notebooks, pens, and a letter attached to a partial manuscript with a note scribbled in red ink:

For the tenth and final time: I do not do collaborations. This is no longer an inquiry. This is harassment, and the proper action will be taken if you don't cease.

Signed, *Geneva Panchella.*

"What is this all about?" I muttered, flipping through the manuscript. I skimmed a paragraph here and there, but it was impossible to piece together what the story was about. The first paragraph read like a dissertation: stale, dry, and completely devoid of the charm and spark that characterized Ginny's writing.

Also stuffed in the bag were dozens of magazine articles about Ginny. Each picture of her had been defaced—eyes blackened, teeth scribbled out, and devil horns drawn on her head. My stomach turned. Was this how someone who claimed to be a devoted fan behaved? Not any fan I'd want to have.

I stuffed everything back into the bag, zipped it up, and slung it over my shoulder. Not only did I need to show it to Kean, but I also wanted my stuff back: the bulldog stickers, the cool yellow pen with the black tassel on top—my entire goodie bag.

Taking a deep breath, I picked up the hem of the curtain and slipped behind it.

Quietly and deliberately, I moved with my shoulders hunched forward, my chin tucked down, and my hands bent at the elbows to gently part the curtains. I crept along, watching each step carefully to ensure I didn't disturb the fabric. My ears were tuned for any reaction from the audience, but it seemed all eyes were glued to Ginny on the stage.

My mind swirled. Corine had seemed so kind and genuine. But she was a thief, and worse, her duffle bag contained some truly disturbing items. It was the kind of thing that might keep a criminal profiler busy for weeks.

"Where are you going with my stuff?" a raspy voice hissed from ahead.

Startled, I snapped my head up and saw Corine blocking my path to Kean. She stood with her arms crossed, her expression dark. My pulse raced as I stretched out my right arm to part the curtain slightly. Corine was cutting me off.

I cleared my throat, preparing to respond, but instinctively raised my index finger to my lips, eyes wide and innocent. Silently, I pointed toward the stage, gesturing to the ongoing talk. Her gaze followed, and for a moment, I hoped the distraction would buy me the time I needed to reach Kean.

"Where are you going with my stuff?" Corine yelled, her voice echoing through the backstage area. She didn't care who heard her. The auditorium grew eerily silent, and I realized everyone had heard her outburst. Before I could process what was happening, Corine narrowed her eyes and bolted toward me.

I'm not ashamed to admit it. I turned tail and ran like the lone survivor in a zombie movie. Windmilling my arms, I shoved past the curtains and broke free into the open wings of the stage. My first instinct was to glance over my shoulder, but the sound of her gym shoes pounding the wooden floor behind me made me think better of it. My best option was to get out the way I'd come in.

Within seconds, I was in the high school corridor. The lobby was to my right, but I turned left, sprinting down the hallway. There had to be somewhere to hide. Each classroom door I tried was locked. I veered down a hallway lined with lockers, then darted into a small alcove with two doors. One read *Counselor Reggie Higgins*. The other said *Boys Room*.

I tried the counselor's door first. Locked, of

course. With no other choice, I slipped into the boys' bathroom. The lights flickered on as I pushed the door open, the motion sensors kicking in. The air was chilly, and the sharp scent of pine cleaner stung my nose. There was nowhere to go but the stalls. Tiptoeing to the furthest one, I shoved the duffle bag behind my back, climbed onto the toilet, and waited.

It felt like I crouched there for half an hour. My breath came shallow as I strained to hear any sign of Corine outside. That's when it hit me. What a stupid move it was to duck in here. There was no escape. Even if I screamed, it was possible no one would hear me. I took a couple of deep breaths to calm myself, but the lights flicked off. The motion sensors, sensing no activity, assumed the room was empty.

The room plunged into pitch-black silence. My clammy hands braced against the stall walls as sweat trickled down my back. My thighs and calves burned from holding the crouching position, and I made a mental note to get in better shape if I survived this. This was above and beyond the call of duty for a front desk clerk at a cozy small town inn. The absurdity of it almost made me laugh.

Just then, the door creaked open, and the lights

flickered on again. My heart leapt into my throat. Someone had come in. My ears strained, picking up the sound of gym shoes shuffling across the tile floor. Corine. She had to know this was the last place I could be.

If only I had a weapon. A bazooka or a machete would be nice, but all I had was a duffle bag stuffed with stolen stickers, defaced magazines, a rejected manuscript, and bad vibes. Fine. That would have to do.

I stayed stone still, my muscles screaming in protest. The strap of the duffle bag dug into my shoulder, pulling me off balance. I held my breath as the shuffling grew louder. Corine was waiting for me to make a sound—a sneeze, a cough, anything to give away my position. The lights flicked off again, plunging us back into darkness.

Using the cover of darkness, I slowly crept off the toilet, moving inch by inch to avoid making noise. My heart pounded as I steadied myself, then leapt out of the stall with the duffle bag raised like a shield. The lights snapped on just as I barreled forward, letting out a battle cry. I collided with someone and knocked us both to the ground.

But it wasn't Corine.

It was a terrified teenage boy, no older than fifteen.

"What?" I blurted, stunned.

"I'm sorry! Don't hurt me!" he stammered, his hands raised in surrender.

"I'm not going to hurt you," I muttered, quickly scrambling to my feet. The boy remained on the ground, still holding his hands up as if I were wielding a weapon.

"Do you know you're in the boys' bathroom?" he asked, wide-eyed.

"Yes." Rolling my eyes, I slung the duffle bag over my shoulder. "Are you hurt? Did you hit your head?"

"No," he replied.

"Okay." I grabbed the door handle, yanked it open, and stepped out into the hallway. What in the world had gotten into me? I'd just tackled a teenager. He'd probably be terrified of public restrooms for the rest of his life because of me.

Before I could dwell on my guilt, I caught a glimpse of David walking past the alcove. He didn't look my way, just strolled down the corridor like he had all the time in the world. At the end of the hall-way, Kean appeared out of nowhere. The two men locked eyes, tension crackling in the air. After a long moment, David turned and bolted.

"Call the police!" Kean shouted as he sprinted past me in pursuit. For a short guy with a spare tire, David could really run.

For a second, I forgot about Corine and the duffle bag. But when I saw her emerge into the lobby at the opposite end of the hallway, it all came rushing back. Which of us would reach the auditorium doors first? It had to be me. It just had to.

Chapter 15

I ran as fast as I could. It wasn't fair. Corine always wore gym shoes and yoga pants, and it was obvious she was in better shape than me. But I clenched my teeth and pushed forward, reaching the auditorium door just as she did. Grabbing the handle, I yanked it open, only for her to clutch the strap of the duffle bag, her nails scratching my shoulder in the process.

"Get off me!" I scowled, holding tight to the bag.

"Give me my bag!" Corine yelled.

"No!"

"Give it to me!"

"Never!" I screamed. "Ginny!"

We were locked in a tug-of-war when Ginny finally appeared from the stage, flanked by Christine and a couple of high school students.

"She's after you, Ginny! Corine is after you!" I shouted, breathless. Before I could say anything else, Corine released the strap, and I tumbled backward into a stack of stage props. She darted back out the door. Ginny rushed to my side as Christine and the students stood frozen in disbelief.

"Are you all right?" Ginny asked, helping me to my feet.

"I've been better," I said, still clutching the strap of the duffle bag. "You need to look inside this bag."

"Isn't that Corine's bag?" Ginny asked, her tone skeptical. "She lugs that thing around like it's a toddler. I have a Louis Vuitton I don't clutch with such intensity," she added with a small chuckle. "I don't think we should go through her things. That's private."

"Oh, you're going to want to," I replied, dropping the bag at her feet. "It was left open. I almost tripped over it. You need to see what's inside. And we need to call the police."

Ginny's eyebrows furrowed as she knelt down—

elegantly, even in three-inch heels and a skin-tight dress—and unzipped the bag. The first thing she pulled out was the same thing I'd noticed earlier: the bulldog sticker in a bumblebee costume.

"These are from my gift bags," she said, her voice laced with disbelief. "They were custom-made, and…" Her voice trailed off as she reached deeper into the bag, retrieving one of the defaced articles. I watched as her confident demeanor faltered, her eyes scanning the crude markings and hateful scribbles. For the first time since I'd met her, the air of invincibility she carried had vanished. She looked heartbroken.

"Ginny, I think we need to get you out of here," I said softly. "She's still out there running around, and that's not all." I took a deep breath. "David is here too. I saw him. I went to follow him, and that's when everything went south with Corine."

Ginny's face darkened. "Her name isn't Corine," she said. "It's Nancy. Nancy Moses. She's been contacting me, my agent, my secretary, my gardener—anyone she can reach—trying to convince me we need to write together. I've been getting threats from her for months. Up until now, I thought she might have been a creation of my ex-husband's. That maybe he was trying to scare me into taking him back. I never thought…"

"I think we should get you back to the inn and…"

Ginny put up her hand, cutting me off mid-sentence.

"Nope. Christine, make yourself useful and tell everyone I'll be right back out there to continue my talk," Ginny ordered. Christine bristled but obeyed, hurrying off to relay the message.

"Ginny, both Corine—or Nancy, or whoever she is—and your ex-husband are roaming the halls of this school. I know Kean is out there, but he's one man with a recent head injury and…"

At the mention of Kean, Ginny's eyes widened. It was like she'd forgotten about him. She placed a hand to her chest, and despite her high heels, she hurried to the backstage door. Pushing it open without hesitation, she ran off in search of Kean, completely unfazed by any danger. I had no choice but to follow her.

We hadn't gone ten paces before we saw Kean standing over both David and Corine—or Nancy—who were sprawled on the floor groaning.

"What did you do?" Ginny shouted.

"Nothing," Kean replied, exasperated. "This numbskull was strolling around like he owned the place. When he saw me, he turned tail like a coward and started running. He plowed right into this lady, and I swear I heard their heads clunk." He tapped David's shoe with his thick boot.

David was clutching his head, his large belly heaving as he struggled to catch his breath. Corine —or Nancy—was also holding her head, groaning softly. Within seconds, Christine reappeared with her entourage of students, and they gasped in unison at the scene before them.

"Why are you just standing there, Christine? Call the police," Ginny barked.

"No!" Corine/Nancy shouted, sounding like a drunken sailor who had just tumbled down a flight of stairs. She jiggled and swayed into a sitting position.

"Oh, okay. Since you said no, I won't call the police," Ginny snapped, her voice dripping with sarcasm. She took two steps closer to Corine/Nancy, her beautifully manicured red index finger pointing down at her. "Are you out of your mind? Shut up and stay put, or so help me, you're going to find my size six heel so far up your..."

"Ginny," I interrupted, jerking my head toward

the students who were staring in wide-eyed shock. Ginny cleared her throat, smoothed the front of her dress, and let out a long, dramatic sigh.

"And you! What do you have to say for yourself?" she demanded, glaring at her ex-husband.

"I'm only here because I love you! I love you, Geneva Lorraine Panchella!" David wailed, his tone dripping with melodrama. The sheer intensity of it made me cringe. I was embarrassed for him.

Ginny, however, looked down at him like he was a piece of gum stuck to the sidewalk. Her eyes narrowed, her nose wrinkled, and her mouth hung slightly open in disbelief. "My middle name is Laverne, you clown!" she snapped. From where I was standing, it looked like Ginny might punch David in the face.

Before things could escalate, Kean stepped in, positioning himself protectively between David and Ginny. His arm circled her waist, guiding her gently backward. His calm presence seemed to defuse the immediate tension. Meanwhile, David's wails had begun to draw a crowd. Curious attendees from Ginny's talk trickled out of the auditorium, lining the walls of the lobby and corridors, eager for a front-row seat to the drama. Thankfully, before anything further could happen, the police arrived.

"I need to finish my talk," Ginny explained to the officers. "These folks paid good money to hear me. It won't take long, and I'll come to the station immediately afterward."

"Ginny! Geneva, my love! Don't do this! I know you still love me!" David howled as the officers cuffed him. Tears streamed down his face as he began to weep uncontrollably. The officers, showing surprising patience, left one uniformed officer at the school to ensure no further disruptions.

Corine—or Nancy—was a stark contrast to David. As the police questioned her, she remained silent, her tight-lipped glare shifting between Ginny and me. Her jaw muscles pulsed as if she were chewing gum, though her mouth was empty. The coldness in her demeanor was unnerving.

"Take a look in that duffle bag," Ginny said, her red lips pressed into a thin line. The officers complied, uncovering not only the marked-up articles and the rejected manuscript but also items I hadn't noticed earlier. A hammer that could have easily been used to destroy Ginny's vintage Fury, and a loaded .22 pistol, were found inside. The fingerprints on the gun matched Corine's—or Nancy's—sealing her fate.

Once the police departed and the onlookers

returned to their seats in the auditorium, Ginny took to the stage again. She explained the chaotic series of events with her usual flair and ended her talk with a perfectly apt statement: "Fact is always stranger than fiction."

I couldn't have agreed more.

Chapter 16

The police officer who stayed with us at the school drove Ginny and me to the police station. I didn't want to go. After the day's excitement, I would have given almost anything for a cup of peppermint tea and a hot bath. But Ginny insisted.

"You must come. You found her bag. The police are going to want to talk to you, too," she said. She was right, of course. They'd want to hear my side of things. Still, I felt like I was in a movie. Ever since leaving the city—where my life had been a routine punctuated by one erratic individual—and moving to the sleepy town of Sierra Hills, I'd found myself in more excitement and drama than I'd ever imagined.

Ginny walked into the police station ahead of me and shot a glare at Corine—or Nancy—who was handcuffed to one side of a metal bench bolted to the floor. David occupied the other side but seemed preoccupied with watching the clock.

I glanced around, surprised at how pleasant the station was. I'd expected drab walls, mismatched metal desks, black cradle telephones, and stacks of files cluttering every surface. Instead, the space was almost serene. Moss-colored walls, the aroma of brewing coffee, and a soft bench in the waiting area made me pause. The plaque on the bench said that it had been dedicated by Mrs. Vivian Lyson over ten years ago. I wondered if she'd been a regular visitor for some reason.

"Miss Panchella, would you come over here, please?" An officer waved Ginny toward a dark brown wooden desk that was as tidy as a pin. He gestured for Ginny and Kean to sit. Meanwhile, I stayed on the bench, making a point not to look in Corine/Nancy's direction.

Just then, Detective Connor appeared. He exchanged a few words with Ginny and Kean before turning his focus to me. As he strolled over, I suddenly felt hot and nervous, like I'd done something wrong.

"Miss Grant, I'm starting to think trouble likes to follow you," he said, his expression unreadable. I couldn't tell if he was being friendly or if he was suspicious and thought I was involved somehow. He waved me over, and I reluctantly followed him to his office. Thankfully, he left the door open.

His office was as neat as the rest of the station. Behind his desk were rows of plaques and awards for his service to the community. The display made me feel dwarfed as I took a seat in front of his desk.

"Do you want to tell me what happened?" he asked, reaching into a mini fridge behind his desk. He pulled out a bottle of water and handed it to me. I took it gratefully, unscrewed the cap, and drank half of it like I'd been stranded in a desert. Then, after a deep breath, I told him everything from my perspective.

Detective Connor listened intently, jotting down notes on a yellow legal pad. His handwriting looked like chicken scratch. When I finished, he looked up at me and asked, "Is that all?"

"Yes. I think I've covered everything," I muttered.

Detective Connor took a deep breath and nodded. "You're free to go."

I sat there for a second, unsure of what I'd

expected him to say. A "good job" or a "I know that had to be scary" would have been nice. But there was nothing. Clearing my throat, I stood and walked out of his office.

Ginny and Kean were still deep in conversation with the police officer. I glanced around and realized no one was paying any attention to me. Quietly, I slipped out of the station and started walking back to the inn. I'd barely made it half a block when a familiar vehicle came into view—Jesse's beat-up Jeep. He pulled up beside me and stopped.

"I was hoping I'd catch you. Detective Connor just called. Said you were here. What in the world happened?" he asked, pushing open the passenger door from the inside.

Climbing in, I sighed. "You won't believe it," I said, launching into the day's events. As I recounted the story for Jesse, I watched his eyes widen in disbelief. Even as I said it, I could barely believe it myself.

"My gosh, Sophie. Were you scared?" he asked, his voice low with concern.

"Of course, I was scared!" I exclaimed. "I can't believe Corine put on such a show, acting like she adored Ginny and wanted to learn from her. What she really wanted was to kill her. And why? That's the part I can't wrap my head around. I have my suspicions, but it's all so weird."

By the time we reached the inn, Jesse still looked shell-shocked. Inside, I had to repeat the entire story again to Stella and Max, explaining that Corine would not be settling her tab since she'd be spending the night in jail. They were just as shocked as Jesse had been.

"You poor thing," Stella cooed, her voice full of sympathy. "You must be exhausted. What an ordeal. Have you had anything to eat?"

"I'll fix you something," Jesse insisted, darting to the kitchen before I could protest.

Max shook his head, a smirk tugging at his lips. "I don't know what it is about you that seems to attract trouble," he teased, his eyes twinkling with amusement.

"That's what Detective Connor said," I muttered, rolling my eyes.

"Max, don't tease her," Stella chided gently. "She's had a long day. Why don't you head to your room and get some rest, dear? Jesse will have room service bring you your food. You've got to be exhausted."

Her motherly tone was impossible to argue

with, so I nodded, murmured my thanks, and made my way upstairs, grateful for a moment of quiet.

I glanced at Max, arching my right eyebrow as his mother came to my defense. He smiled and chuckled, but quickly regained his more serious expression. Despite myself, I smiled back. I wanted to laugh but refused to give him the satisfaction. How dare he be so charming and pleasant after all I'd been through?

Stella insisted on escorting me to my room. I wanted to wait up for Ginny and Kean to return and find out what had happened, but after my food arrived and I went through the soothing ritual of a hot shower, I collapsed onto the bed. It wasn't even eight o'clock.

When I woke up again at eleven, I was wide awake. I flipped through the channels, but there was nothing worth watching, not that I was much of a TV person to begin with. I tried to read Ginny's book, but my mind wouldn't focus. How many times could I reread the same paragraph?

Finally, I decided to check on Ginny. Wrapping myself in my robe over my pajamas, I shuffled silently down the hallway to her room at the far end of the building. Before knocking, I pressed my ear to the door but heard nothing. My toes, bare on the cold floor, ached in protest. I should have worn socks.

Taking a deep breath, I knocked softly. Nothing stirred. I knocked a little louder but still got no answer. Could they still be at the police station after all this time? Maybe they'd gone out to grab something to eat. That had to be it.

Still restless, I decided to walk to the lobby. The fireplace was probably crackling, and Stella sometimes put out chocolate chip cookies for late-arriving guests. Gary, the night manager, would be at the desk. I rarely saw him since he worked the eleven-to-seven shift. He was an older man, retired, with a kind demeanor.

"Hello, Sophie," he greeted me warmly, his voice carrying the softness of a grandparent.

"Hi, Gary," I replied.

"Can't sleep?"

"No, just thought I'd take a walk and sit by the fire for a few minutes," I said with a smile.

"I've got something here for you," he said, retrieving an envelope from under the counter. "That woman writer left it for you."

"Left it? Did she check out?" I asked, surprised.

"She did. Her and that big bald fella. They left about twenty minutes ago," Gary explained.

Taking the envelope, I walked over to the fire and settled into a chair to read it. Ginny's handwriting was as elegant as she was. Even her curse words, which she wrote just as she spoke them, looked graceful, like they belonged in a frame. The note read:

Dear Sophie,

It was such a long day that the news of my car being ready made me want to shake the dust of this town off my shoes and head out to somewhere new.

David and I came to an agreement. If I gave him my Plymouth Fury along with an additional ten thousand dollars spending cash, he'd leave me alone forever. I knew he just wanted a few more dollars. I could have nipped it in the bud if I hadn't been so stubborn. The police let him go, and I didn't press any charges against my stupid ex-husband.

As for Nancy Moses, she was responsible for vandalizing my car, sneaking up on Kean, almost running us off the road when we first arrived, and a host of other things I'd blamed on David. It seems she thought that she and I were destined to write together. But I'd read her work, and to say she needed help was being kind. She just wasn't a writer. So, since she couldn't join me, she was going to beat me.

There will be a trial, and she'll be going away for a long time. But it makes for a good story, don't you think?

I hope you aren't mad at me for leaving this way. It has truly been a joy getting to know you, and I will forever call you a friend. As such, I put all my dearest constituents in my novels. So, when my next book comes out, the one that takes place at an inn similar to a place we both know, look for yourself.

In the meantime, Kean and I are heading off to Las Vegas. I wonder what we are going to do when we get there?

XXOO,

Ginny

I FOLDED the letter and slipped it back into the envelope. With the fire crackling warmly beside me, I sat for a few more minutes, watching the flames dance and leap with every soft breeze that swept across the chimney top. My thoughts drifted to Ginny's book signing and her writing workshop. A small smile tugged at my lips as I wondered if, perhaps, I might take a stab at writing something myself. Maybe.

About the Author

Harper Lin is a 3x *USA TODAY* bestselling cozy mystery author. When she's not reading or writing mysteries, she loves going to yoga classes, hiking, and baking with her family and friends.

For a complete list of her books by series, visit her website.

www.HarperLin.com